# studio 407

## PRESENTS

# FICTIONAUTS

Written by
**MAURO MANTELLA**
Art by
**LEANDRO RIZZO**
Colors by
**MARCELO BLANCO**
Adaptation by
**CHAD JONES**
Letters by
**LOGAN SWIFT &
MICHAEL SEBASTIAN**
Edited by
**CHAD JONES**

"Fictonauts" is a production of
Altercomics Studio

Altercomics studio
www.altercomics.com.ar

CEO:
**ALEX LEUNG**
Marketing and PR Manager:
**IVAN SALAZAR**
Graphic Design:
**ALAN RAMIREZ**
Production:
**LOGAN SWIFT & ALEXANDRIA BARKER**

FICTIONAUTS Published by Studio 407. First printing 2012. Copyright © 2012 Altercomics Studio. All rights reserved. FICTIONAUTS ™ (including all prominent characters featured herein), logo, and all character likenesses are trademarks of Mauro Mantella, Leandro Rizzo, and Altercomics Studio unless otherwise noted. No part of this publication may be reproduced or transmitted in any form or by any means (except for short excerpts for review purposes), without the express written permission of Studio 407. All characters, stories and incidents mentioned in this publication are entirely fictional. Any similarities to persons living or dead (and undead) are coincidental. Studio 407 is a division of Forty Guns and Seven Swords, LLC. Studio 407 does not accept unsolicited story ideas, stories or artwork. Printed in Korea.

# CHAPTER 1
# KEEP WATCHING THE SEA!

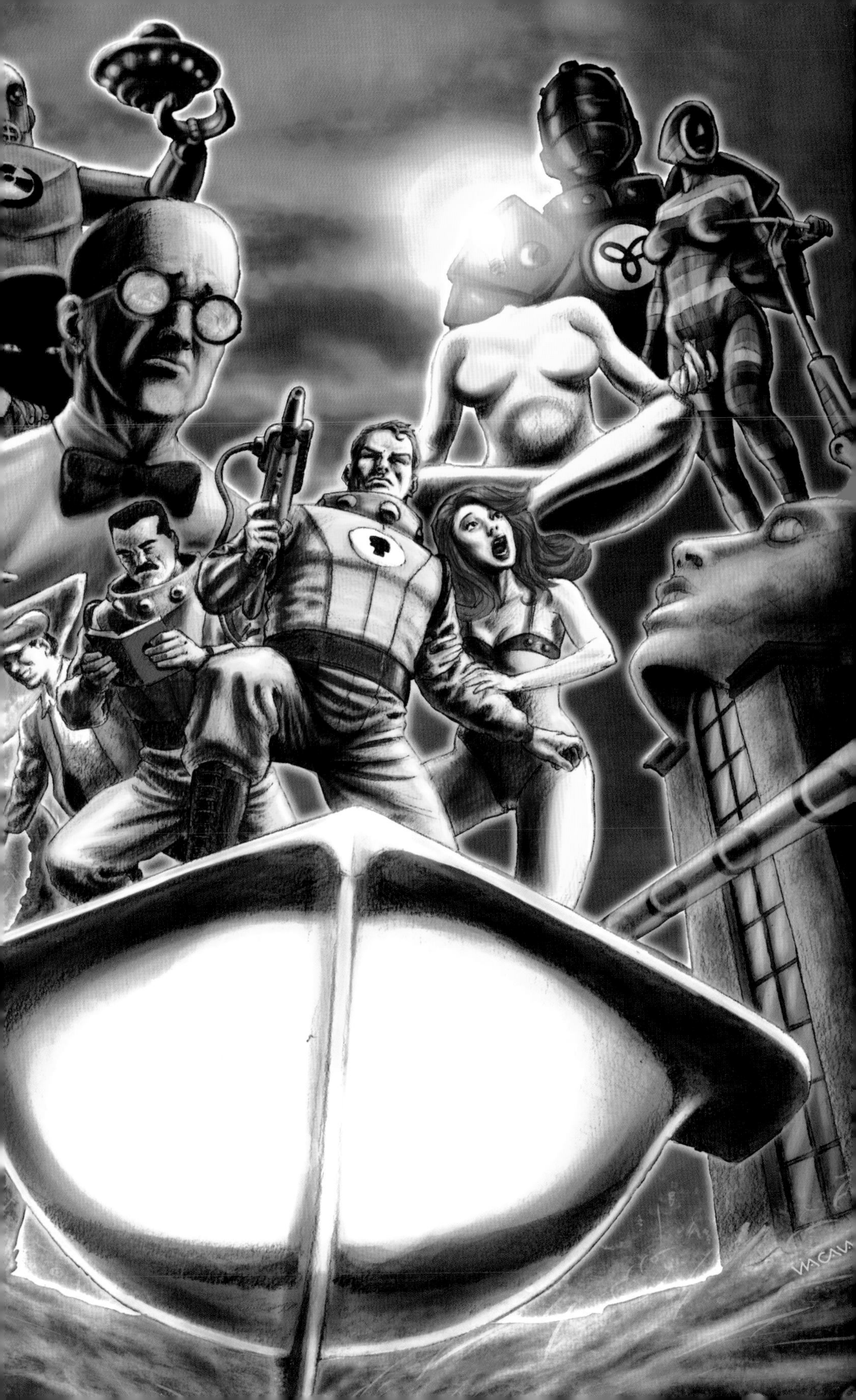

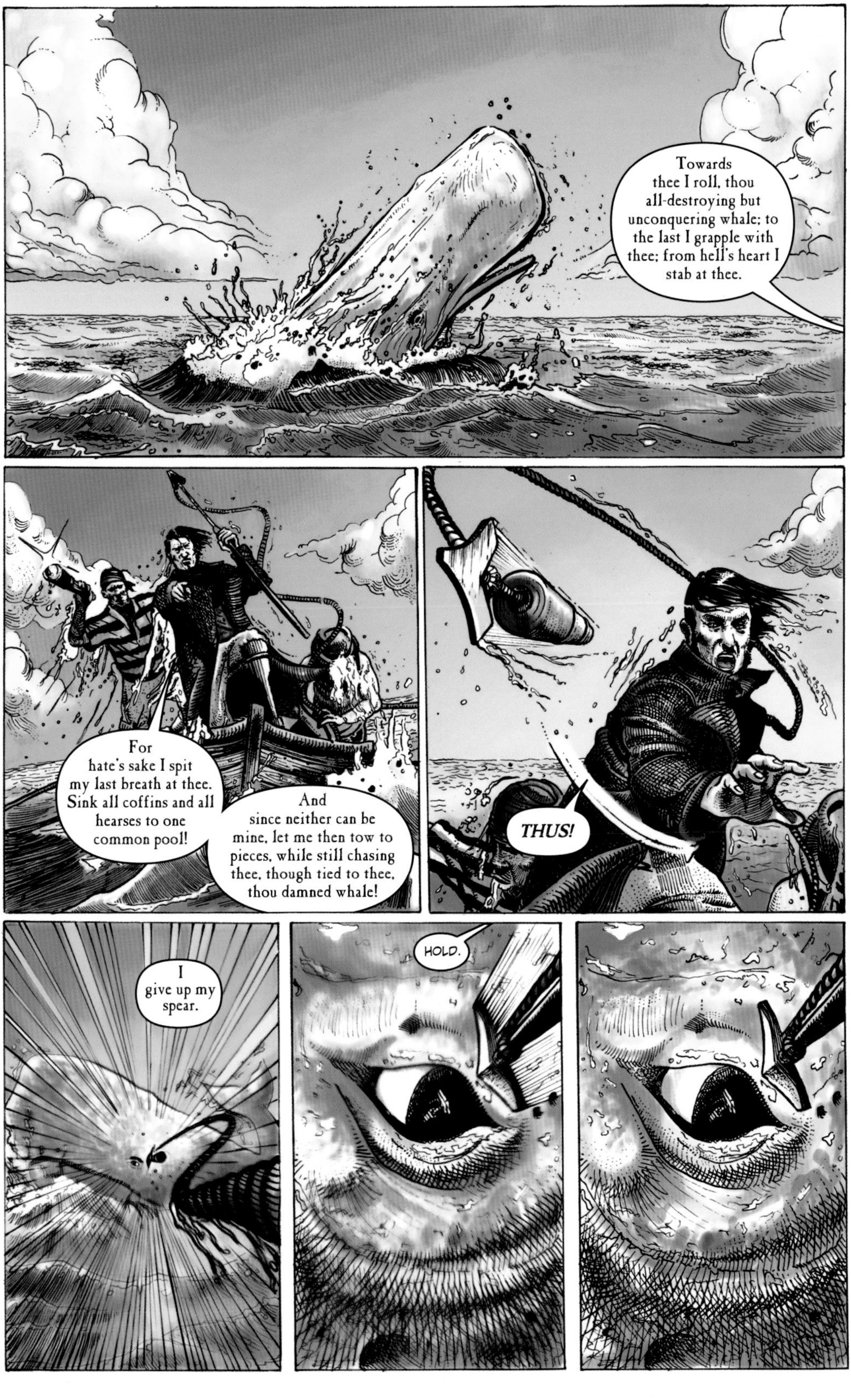
Towards thee I roll, thou all-destroying but unconquering whale; to the last I grapple with thee; from hell's heart I stab at thee.
For hate's sake I spit my last breath at thee. Sink all coffins and all hearses to one common pool!
And since neither can be mine, let me then tow to pieces, while still chasing thee, though tied to thee, thou damned whale!
THUS!
I give up my spear.
HOLD.

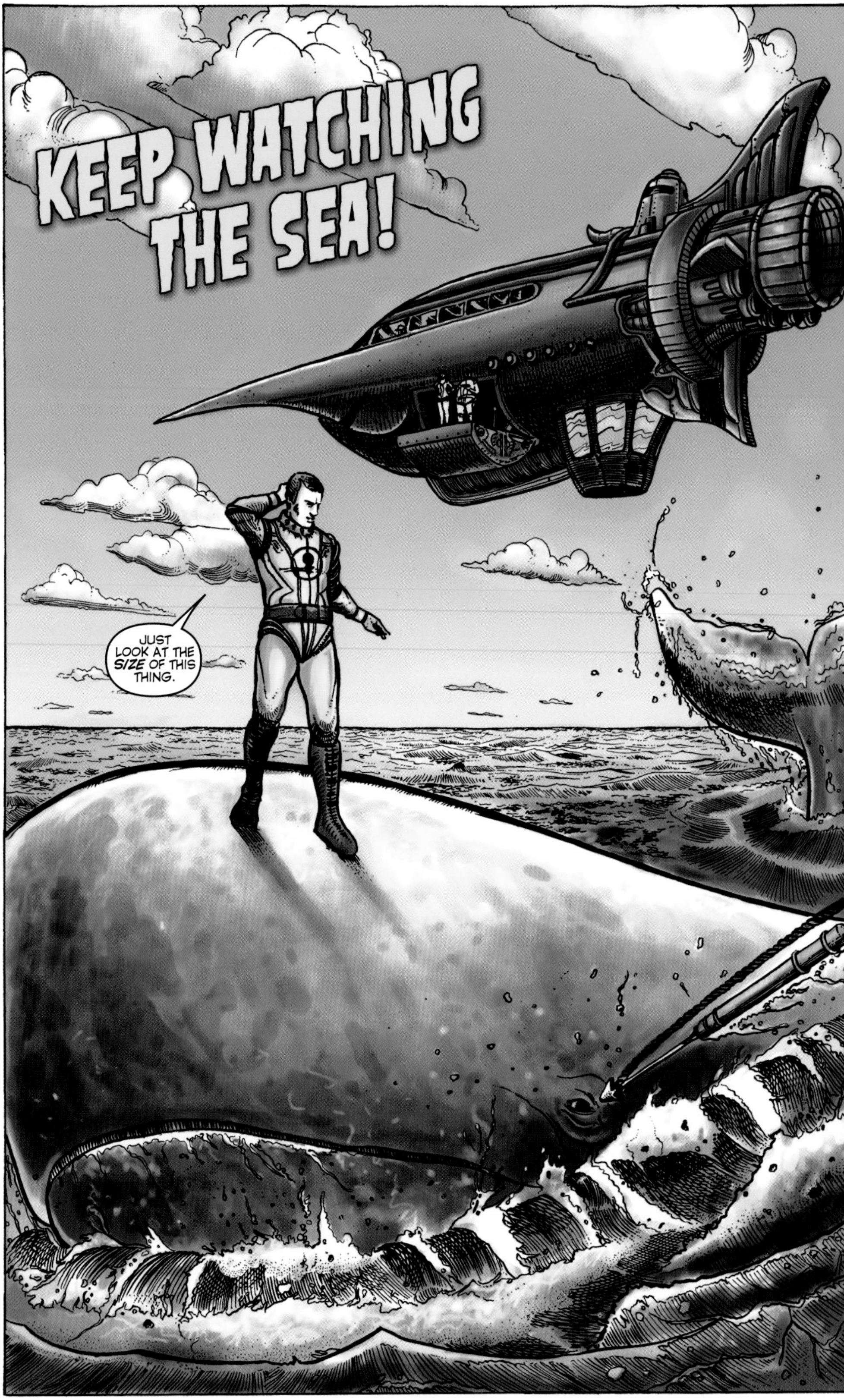
KEEP WATCHING THE SEA!
JUST LOOK AT THE SIZE OF THIS THING.

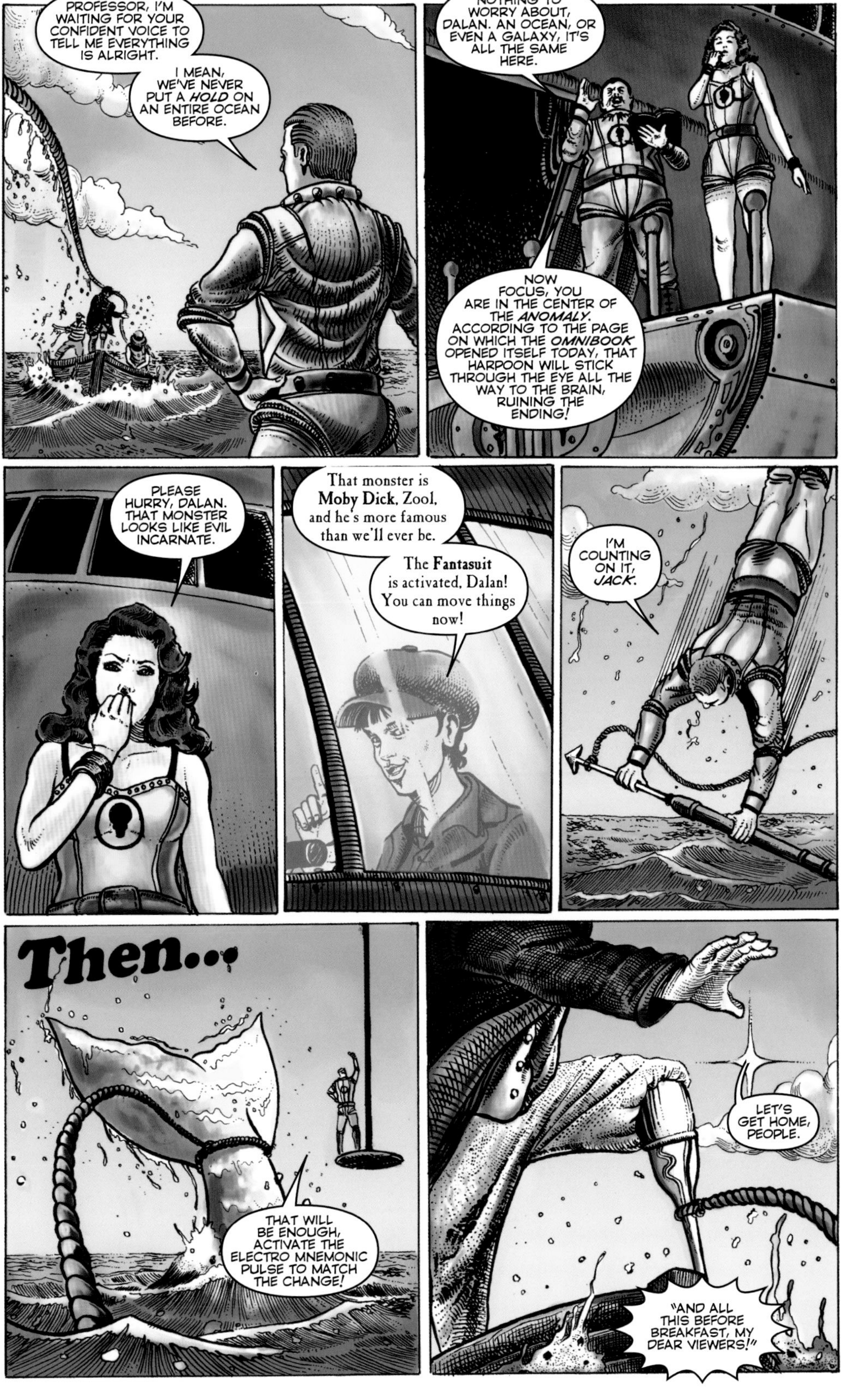
PROFESSOR, I'M WAITING FOR YOUR CONFIDENT VOICE TO TELL ME EVERYTHING IS ALRIGHT.
I MEAN, WE'VE NEVER PUT A HOLD ON AN ENTIRE OCEAN BEFORE.
NOTHING TO WORRY ABOUT, DALAN. AN OCEAN, OR EVEN A GALAXY, IT'S ALL THE SAME HERE.
NOW FOCUS, YOU ARE IN THE CENTER OF THE ANOMALY. ACCORDING TO THE PAGE ON WHICH THE OMNIBOOK OPENED ITSELF TODAY, THAT HARPOON WILL STICK THROUGH THE EYE ALL THE WAY TO THE BRAIN, RUINING THE ENDING!
PLEASE HURRY, DALAN. THAT MONSTER LOOKS LIKE EVIL INCARNATE.
That monster is Moby Dick, Zool, and he's more famous than we'll ever be.
The Fantasuit is activated, Dalan! You can move things now!
I'M COUNTING ON IT, JACK.
Then...
THAT WILL BE ENOUGH, ACTIVATE THE ELECTRO MNEMONIC PULSE TO MATCH THE CHANGE!
LET'S GET HOME, PEOPLE.
"AND ALL THIS BEFORE BREAKFAST, MY DEAR VIEWERS!"

THIS IS THE FANTASTIC LIFE OF *HYPERCITY'S* MOST FAMOUS HEROES, AT LEAST ACCORDING TO THE OPINION OF YOUR HUMBLE HOST, JEFF RUSSEL!

COULD WE ENVY THEM MORE? I WONDER.

COULD A MORE EXCITING JOB EXIST THAN NAVIGATING THROUGH THE WORLDS OF FICTION, HELPING *AUGUSTE DUPIN* TO FOLLOW THE RIGHT LEAD OR HELPING *TARZAN* AVOID GRABBING THE WRONG LIANA?!

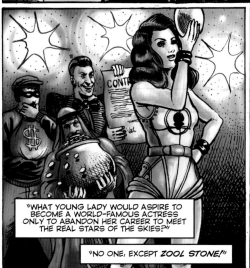

"WHAT YOUNG LADY WOULD ASPIRE TO BECOME A WORLD-FAMOUS ACTRESS ONLY TO ABANDON HER CAREER TO MEET THE REAL STARS OF THE SKIES?"

"NO ONE, EXCEPT *ZOOL STONE!*"

"WHO BUT *PROFESSOR EMERIO STANDFORD* COULD BEFRIEND SHAKESPEARE'S CREATIONS OR DEBATE THE PHILOSOPHY OF MYTH WITH THE MYTHS THEMSELVES?!"

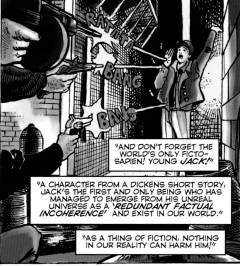

"AND DON'T FORGET THE WORLD'S ONLY FICTO-SAPIEN! YOUNG *JACK!*"

"A CHARACTER FROM A DICKENS SHORT STORY, JACK'S THE FIRST AND ONLY BEING WHO HAS MANAGED TO EMERGE FROM HIS UNREAL UNIVERSE AS A *'REDUNDANT FACTUAL INCOHERENCE'* AND EXIST IN OUR WORLD."

"AS A THING OF FICTION, NOTHING IN OUR REALITY CAN HARM HIM!"

"AND, OF COURSE, LADIES AND GENTLEMEN... *DALAN VALLEY!* THE BRAVEST MAN IN HYPERCITY!"

"THE ATLAS THAT EVERY WOMAN DESIRES AND EVERY MAN ADMIRES."

"AND WE ARE *LIVE* FROM THEIR HEADQUARTERS! I GIVE YOU..."

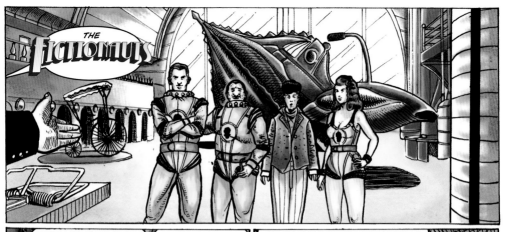

# THE FICTIONAUTS

FIRST, LET ME THANK YOU ON BEHALF OF OUR VIEWING AUDIENCE FOR LETTING ME INTERVIEW YOU HERE. IT'S SUCH AN HONOR.

THE HONOR IS ALL OURS. IT SEEMED THE BEST PLACE TO SHARE OUR ADVENTURES WITH OUR FANS.

AND ALSO FOR THOSE POOR PAPARAZZI, WASTING MONEY BOOKING ROOMS IN NEARBY BUILDINGS.

*HA HA HA!* HOW VERY THOUGHTFUL! BUT TELL US, HOW IMPORTANT IS IT TO CONTINUE WATCHING THE VAST GROUNDS OF FICTION?

FICTION IS A COSMIC REFLECTION OF OUR SUBCONSCIOUS MINDS.

AND IT'S OUR JOB TO MAKE SURE THAT IF SOMETHING GOES WRONG, IT GETS CORRECTED BEFORE THE EFFECTS REACH OUR REALITY. AND THE HEALTH FROM ONE OBVIOUSLY HELPS THE OTHER.

I SEE, BUT YOU HAVEN'T BEEN AROUND FOREVER. WHO WATCHED OVER FICTION BEFORE THE FICTIONAUTS?

THERE HAVE ALWAYS BEEN GUARDIANS, IN ONE FORM OR ANOTHER.

BUT TODAY, FICTION IS EXPANDING AT AN *EXPONENTIAL* RATE. NOT JUST LITERATURE, BUT FILM, RADIO, TELEVISION, WHO KNOWS WHAT'S NEXT!

FICTION IS IN A CONSTANT STATE OF FLUX. STORIES BEGIN TO OVERLAP AND INFLUENCE ONE ANOTHER. THAT'S WHERE WE COME IN.

WE KEEP AN EYE ON THE OMNIBOOK -- GIVEN TO US BY NONE OTHER THAN *LADY CONCEPTIA* OF *IDEOPOLIS* -- BEFORE PROBLEMS GET OUT OF HAND.

THE HAVOC THAT COULD RESULT FROM COLLIDING FICTIONAL ANOMALIES WOULD BE CATASTROPHIC.

FANTASY IS SERIOUS BUSINESS, MY FRIEND. JUST ASK JACK.

Indeed! If it weren't for Captain Valley and the others, I would have ended as a semantic abstraction -- trapped forever between the lines of a Dickens short story!

I SEE...

TELEPHONE

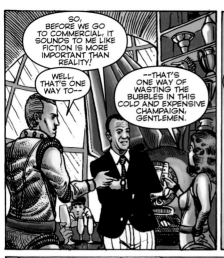

SO, BEFORE WE GO TO COMMERCIAL, IT SOUNDS TO ME LIKE FICTION IS MORE IMPORTANT THAN REALITY!

WELL, THAT'S ONE WAY TO--

--THAT'S ONE WAY OF WASTING THE BUBBLES IN THIS COLD AND EXPENSIVE CHAMPAIGN, GENTLEMEN.

AND IF YOU'LL ALLOW ME A LITTLE ABUSE OF MY WELL-KNOWN VANITY...

THERE'S NOTHING MORE IMPORTANT THAN THE REALITY / LIVE IN, DON'T YOU THINK, BOYS?

HA HA HA HA!

CHEERS TO THAT, ZOOL!

CHEERS TO THAT.

REYNOLDS

ESTAN ENTRE NOSOTROS

HYPERCITY HOME OF THE Fictionauts

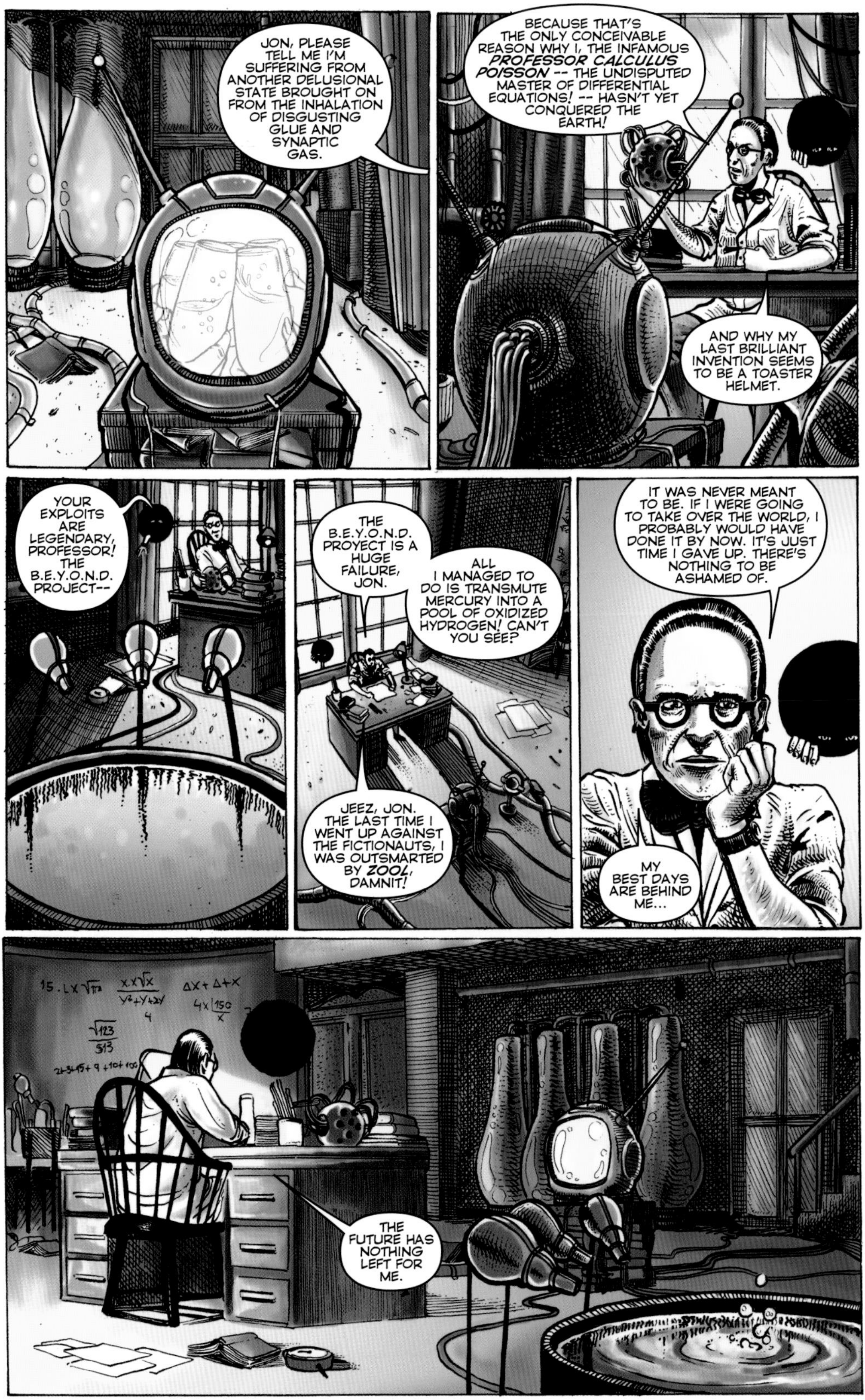
JON, PLEASE TELL ME I'M SUFFERING FROM ANOTHER DELUSIONAL STATE BROUGHT ON FROM THE INHALATION OF DISGUSTING GLUE AND SYNAPTIC GAS.
BECAUSE THAT'S THE ONLY CONCEIVABLE REASON WHY I, THE INFAMOUS ***PROFESSOR CALCULUS POISSON*** -- THE UNDISPUTED MASTER OF DIFFERENTIAL EQUATIONS! -- HASN'T YET CONQUERED THE EARTH!
AND WHY MY LAST BRILLIANT INVENTION SEEMS TO BE A TOASTER HELMET.
YOUR EXPLOITS ARE LEGENDARY, PROFESSOR! THE B.E.Y.O.N.D. PROJECT--
THE B.E.Y.O.N.D. PROYECT IS A HUGE FAILURE, JON.
ALL I MANAGED TO DO IS TRANSMUTE MERCURY INTO A POOL OF OXIDIZED HYDROGEN! CAN'T YOU SEE?
JEEZ, JON. THE LAST TIME I WENT UP AGAINST THE FICTIONAUTS, I WAS OUTSMARTED BY ***ZOOL***, DAMNIT!
IT WAS NEVER MEANT TO BE. IF I WERE GOING TO TAKE OVER THE WORLD, I PROBABLY WOULD HAVE DONE IT BY NOW. IT'S JUST TIME I GAVE UP. THERE'S NOTHING TO BE ASHAMED OF.
MY BEST DAYS ARE BEHIND ME...
THE FUTURE HAS NOTHING LEFT FOR ME.

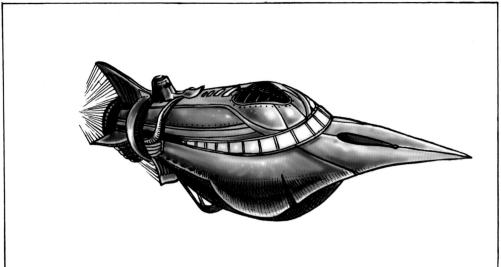

What is it, Professor? Did Zool wash a dish?

HILARIOUS, JACK

NO. IT'S ABOUT THE OMNIBOOK... I JUST FOUND *TWO BLANK PAGES.*

I WAS ABOUT TO PUT IT DOWN... WHEN IT OPENED ITSELF ON THEM. IT'S THE FIRST TIME IT'S OPENED TWICE IN LESS THAN TWENTY-FOUR HOURS!

LET'S HOPE *LADY CONCEPTIA* HAS AN EXPLANATION.

LET'S HOPE.

WHY THE LONG FACE, JACK? IS THE MARTINI TOO BITTER?

No, it's... exquisite, really. Maybe I'm just dizzy from the amount of white space out there.

Is it much farther?

IT'S NOT A QUESTION OF 'HOW FAR.'

REMEMBER THAT THROUGH THE SPACE WE DON'T TRAVEL, WE JUST WAIT TO BE DISCERNED.

YOU CAN'T MEASURE DISTANCE IN A CONVENTIONAL SENSE...

BUT HOLD TIGHT, CHUM, WE'LL HIT *IDEOPOLIS* ANY SECOND.

Yes, there it is!

What did you feel the first time you saw it, Dalan?

WELL, I WAS ONLY A FIFTEEN-YEAR-OLD INVENTOR WITH DREAMS OF X-RAY SPECS THAT COULD PEEP AT WOMEN'S UNDERGARMENTS WHEN I FIRST MET A FICTIONAUT, JACK... WITH NO IDEA OF THE ADVENTURE THAT AWAITED ME... SO JUST IMAGINE, JACK.

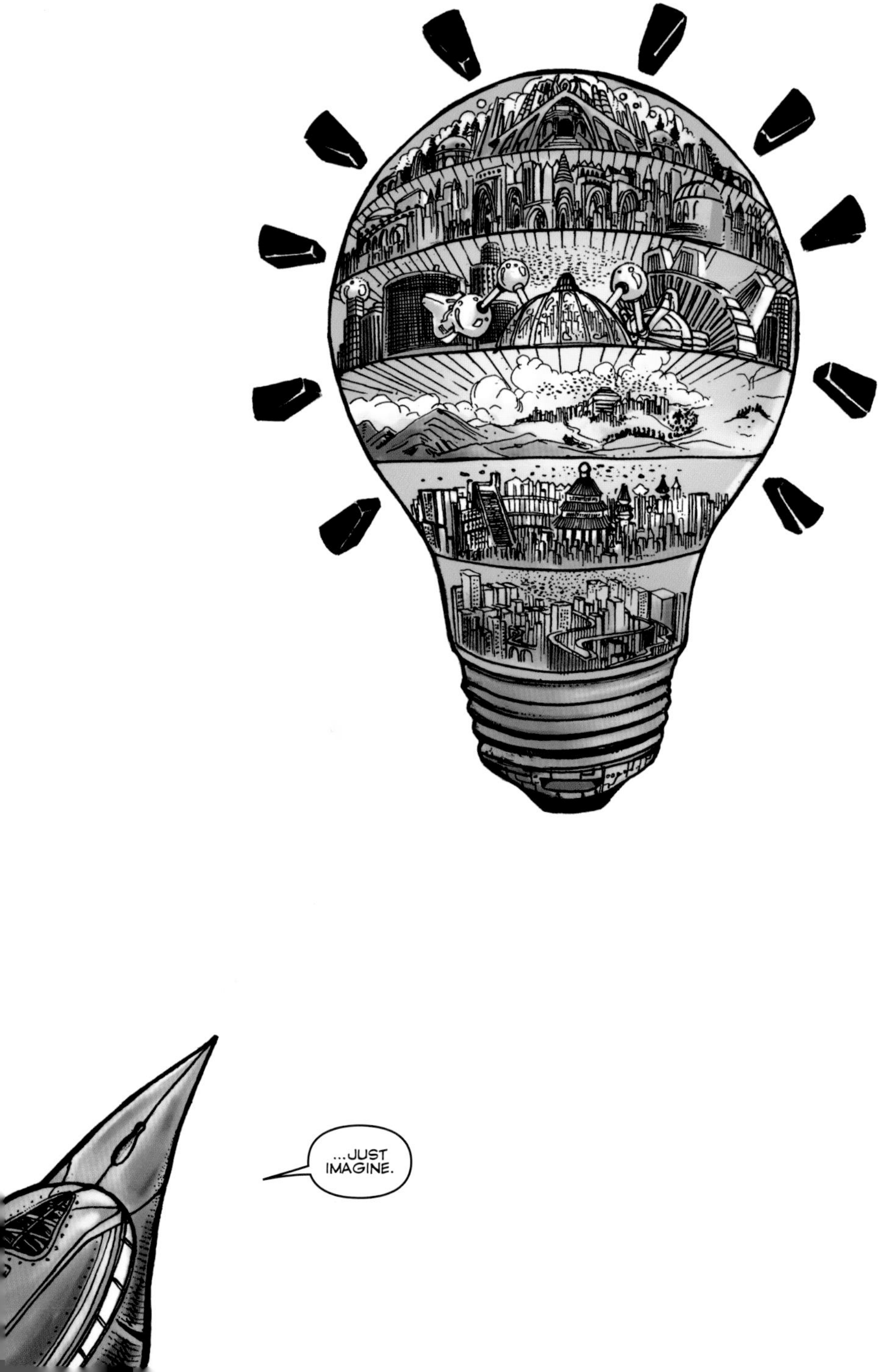
...JUST IMAGINE.

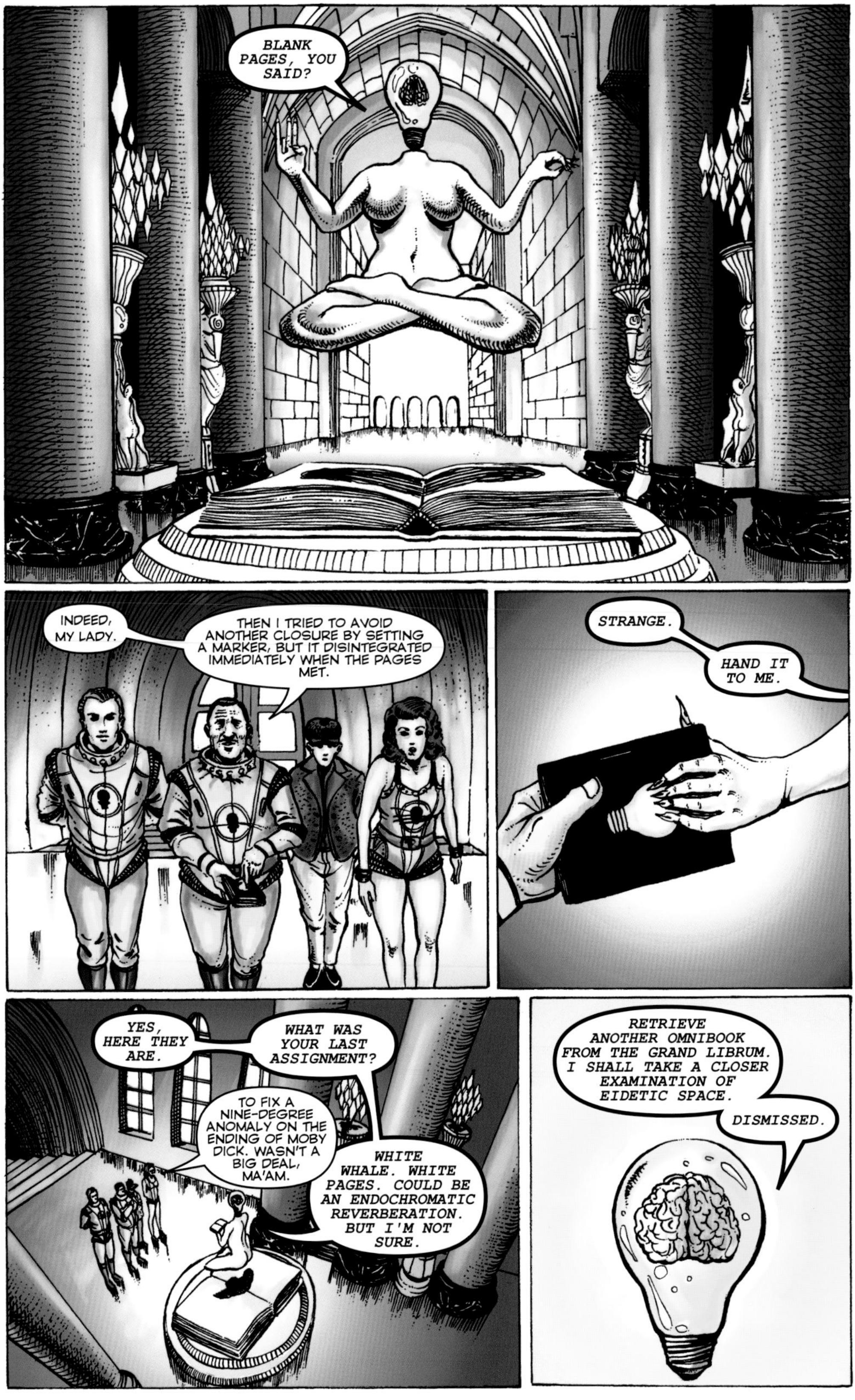
BLANK PAGES, YOU SAID?
INDEED, MY LADY.
THEN I TRIED TO AVOID ANOTHER CLOSURE BY SETTING A MARKER, BUT IT DISINTEGRATED IMMEDIATELY WHEN THE PAGES MET.
STRANGE.
HAND IT TO ME.
YES, HERE THEY ARE.
WHAT WAS YOUR LAST ASSIGNMENT?
TO FIX A NINE-DEGREE ANOMALY ON THE ENDING OF MOBY DICK. WASN'T A BIG DEAL, MA'AM.
WHITE WHALE. WHITE PAGES. COULD BE AN ENDOCHROMATIC REVERBERATION. BUT I'M NOT SURE.
RETRIEVE ANOTHER OMNIBOOK FROM THE GRAND LIBRUM. I SHALL TAKE A CLOSER EXAMINATION OF EIDETIC SPACE.
DISMISSED.

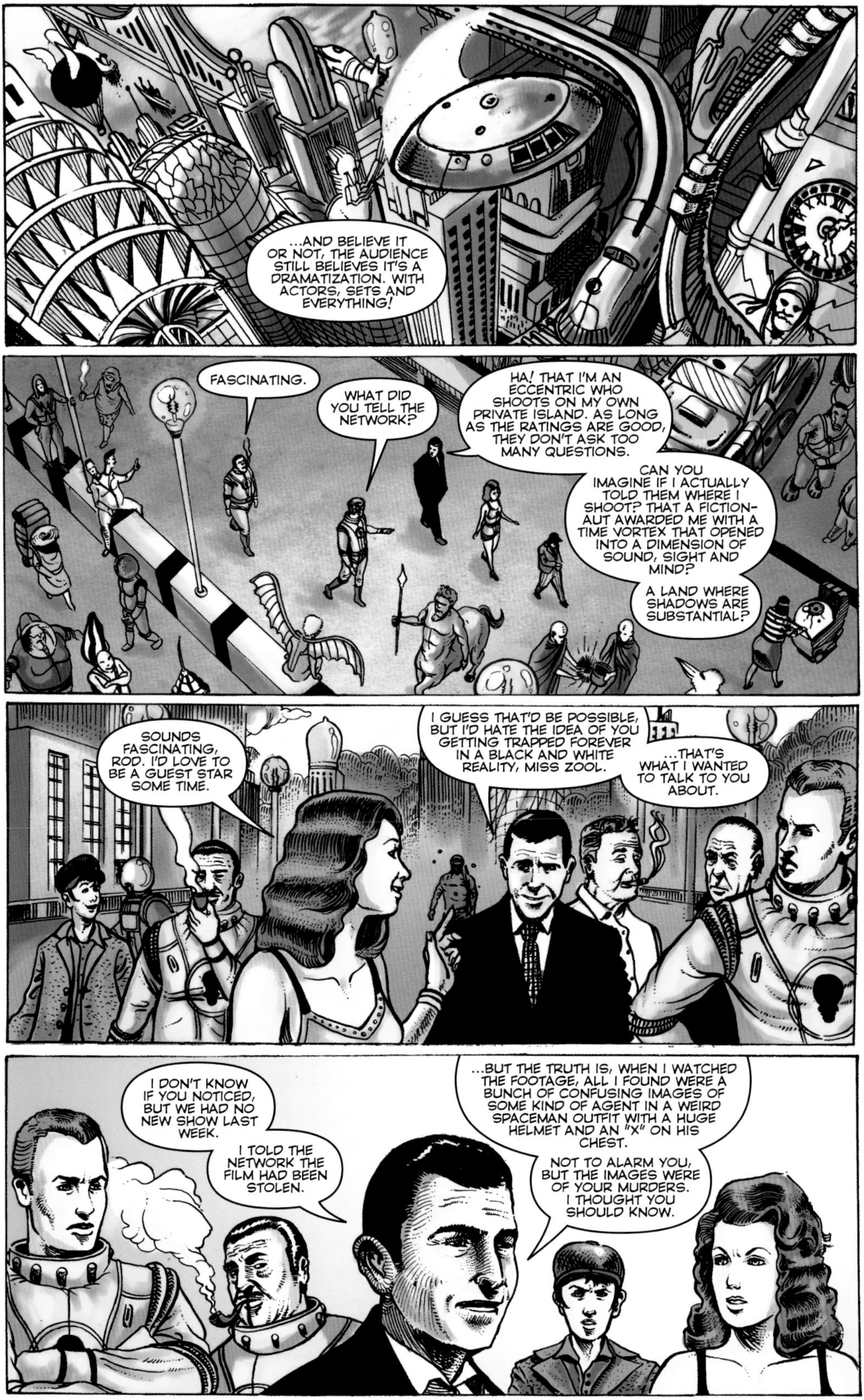
...AND BELIEVE IT OR NOT, THE AUDIENCE STILL BELIEVES IT'S A DRAMATIZATION. WITH ACTORS, SETS AND EVERYTHING!
FASCINATING.
WHAT DID YOU TELL THE NETWORK?
HA! THAT I'M AN ECCENTRIC WHO SHOOTS ON MY OWN PRIVATE ISLAND. AS LONG AS THE RATINGS ARE GOOD, THEY DON'T ASK TOO MANY QUESTIONS.
CAN YOU IMAGINE IF I ACTUALLY TOLD THEM WHERE I SHOOT? THAT A FICTION-AUT AWARDED ME WITH A TIME VORTEX THAT OPENED INTO A DIMENSION OF SOUND, SIGHT AND MIND?
A LAND WHERE SHADOWS ARE SUBSTANTIAL?
SOUNDS FASCINATING, ROD. I'D LOVE TO BE A GUEST STAR SOME TIME.
I GUESS THAT'D BE POSSIBLE, BUT I'D HATE THE IDEA OF YOU GETTING TRAPPED FOREVER IN A BLACK AND WHITE REALITY, MISS ZOOL.
...THAT'S WHAT I WANTED TO TALK TO YOU ABOUT.
I DON'T KNOW IF YOU NOTICED, BUT WE HAD NO NEW SHOW LAST WEEK.
I TOLD THE NETWORK THE FILM HAD BEEN STOLEN.
...BUT THE TRUTH IS, WHEN I WATCHED THE FOOTAGE, ALL I FOUND WERE A BUNCH OF CONFUSING IMAGES OF SOME KIND OF AGENT IN A WEIRD SPACEMAN OUTFIT WITH A HUGE HELMET AND AN "X" ON HIS CHEST.
NOT TO ALARM YOU, BUT THE IMAGES WERE OF YOUR MURDERS. I THOUGHT YOU SHOULD KNOW.

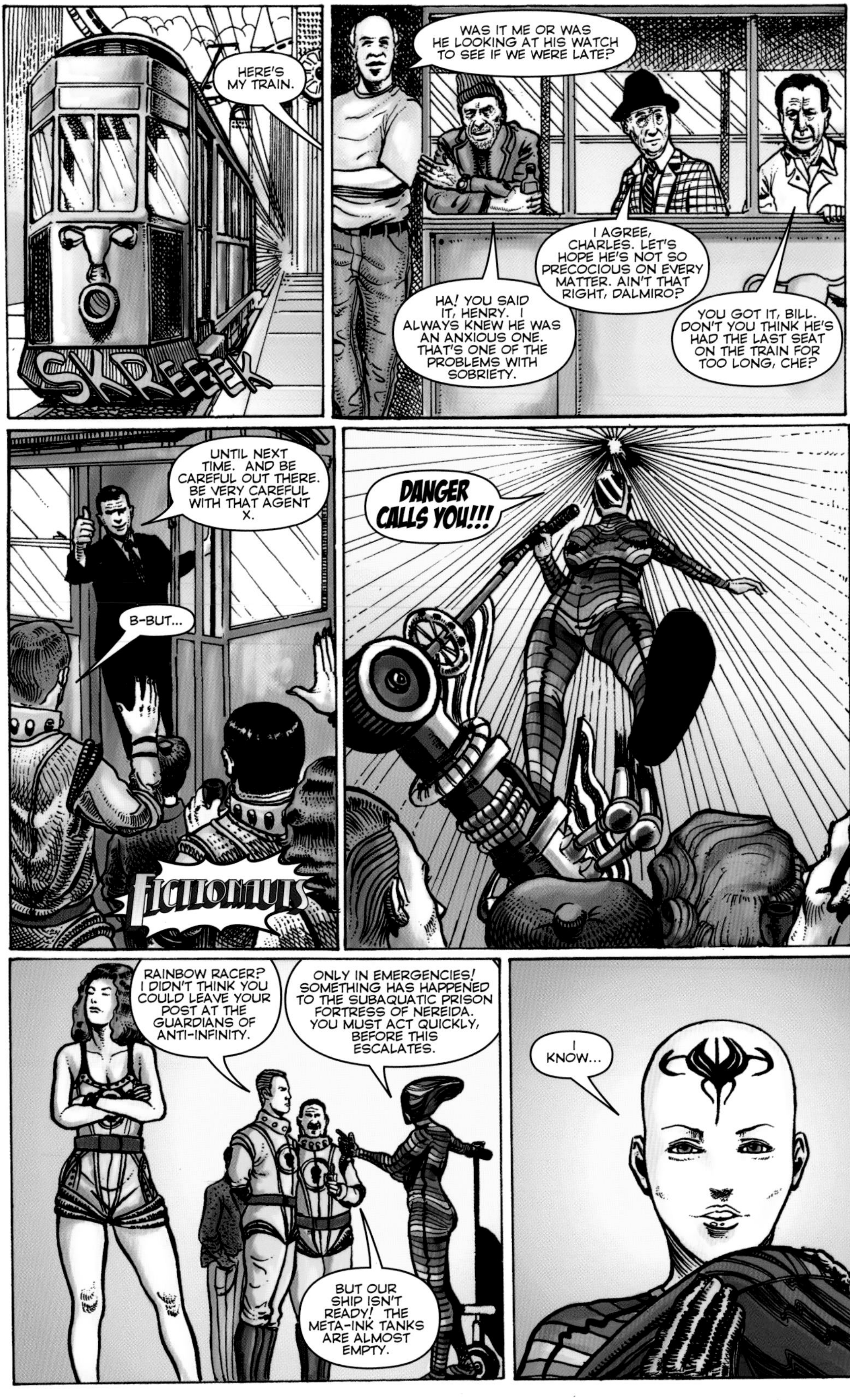
HERE'S MY TRAIN.
SKREEEK
WAS IT ME OR WAS HE LOOKING AT HIS WATCH TO SEE IF WE WERE LATE?
HA! YOU SAID IT, HENRY. I ALWAYS KNEW HE WAS AN ANXIOUS ONE. THAT'S ONE OF THE PROBLEMS WITH SOBRIETY.
I AGREE, CHARLES. LET'S HOPE HE'S NOT SO PRECOCIOUS ON EVERY MATTER. AIN'T THAT RIGHT, DALMIRO?
YOU GOT IT, BILL. DON'T YOU THINK HE'S HAD THE LAST SEAT ON THE TRAIN FOR TOO LONG, CHE?
UNTIL NEXT TIME. AND BE CAREFUL OUT THERE. BE VERY CAREFUL WITH THAT AGENT X.
B-BUT...
FICTIONAUTS
DANGER CALLS YOU!!!
RAINBOW RACER? I DIDN'T THINK YOU COULD LEAVE YOUR POST AT THE GUARDIANS OF ANTI-INFINITY.
ONLY IN EMERGENCIES! SOMETHING HAS HAPPENED TO THE SUBAQUATIC PRISON FORTRESS OF NEREIDA. YOU MUST ACT QUICKLY, BEFORE THIS ESCALATES.
BUT OUR SHIP ISN'T READY! THE META-INK TANKS ARE ALMOST EMPTY.
I KNOW...

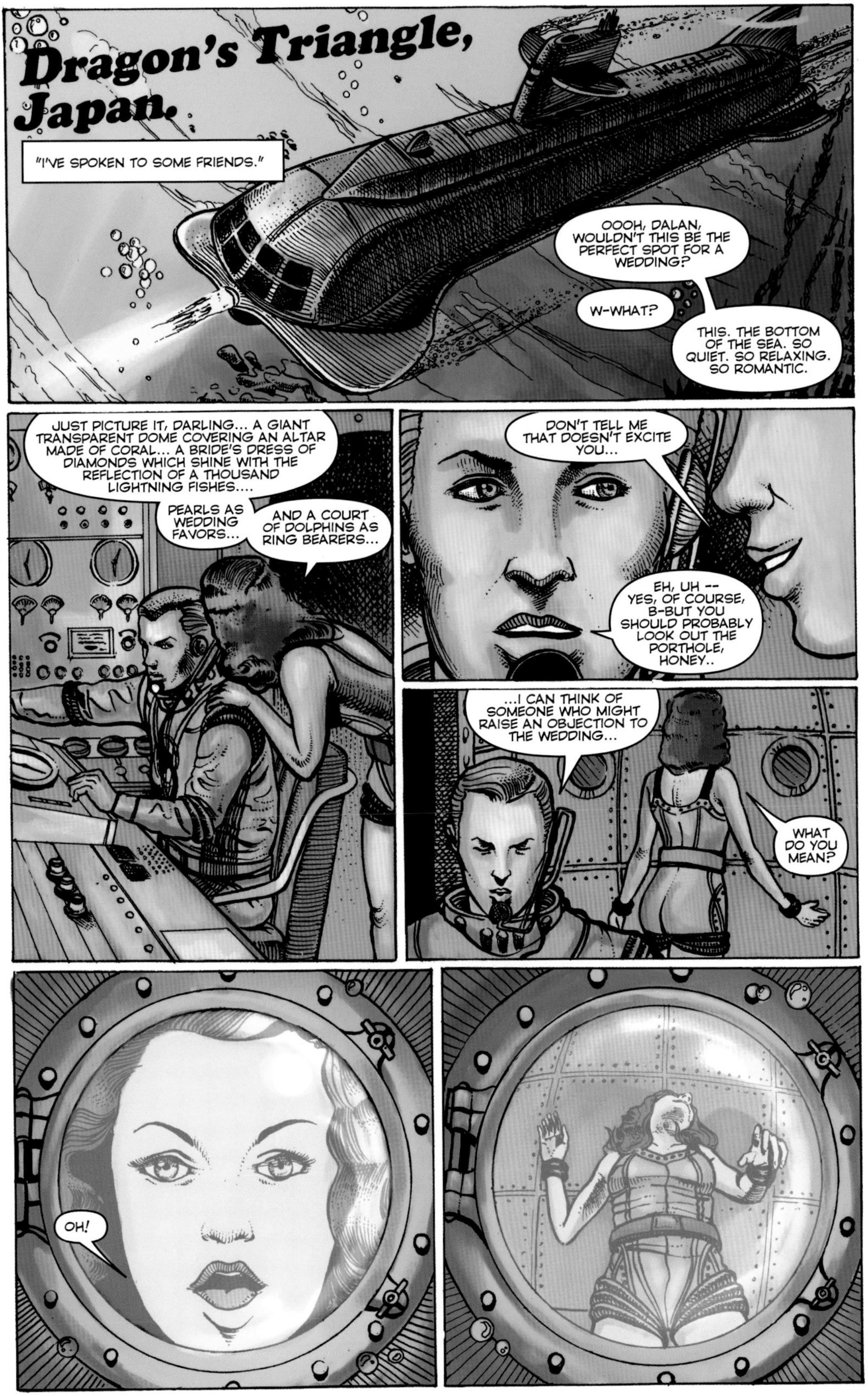
Dragon's Triangle, Japan.
"I'VE SPOKEN TO SOME FRIENDS."
OOOH, DALAN, WOULDN'T THIS BE THE PERFECT SPOT FOR A WEDDING?
W-WHAT?
THIS. THE BOTTOM OF THE SEA. SO QUIET. SO RELAXING. SO ROMANTIC.
JUST PICTURE IT, DARLING... A GIANT TRANSPARENT DOME COVERING AN ALTAR MADE OF CORAL... A BRIDE'S DRESS OF DIAMONDS WHICH SHINE WITH THE REFLECTION OF A THOUSAND LIGHTNING FISHES....
PEARLS AS WEDDING FAVORS...
AND A COURT OF DOLPHINS AS RING BEARERS...
DON'T TELL ME THAT DOESN'T EXCITE YOU...
EH, UH -- YES, OF COURSE, B-BUT YOU SHOULD PROBABLY LOOK OUT THE PORTHOLE, HONEY..
...I CAN THINK OF SOMEONE WHO MIGHT RAISE AN OBJECTION TO THE WEDDING...
WHAT DO YOU MEAN?
OH!

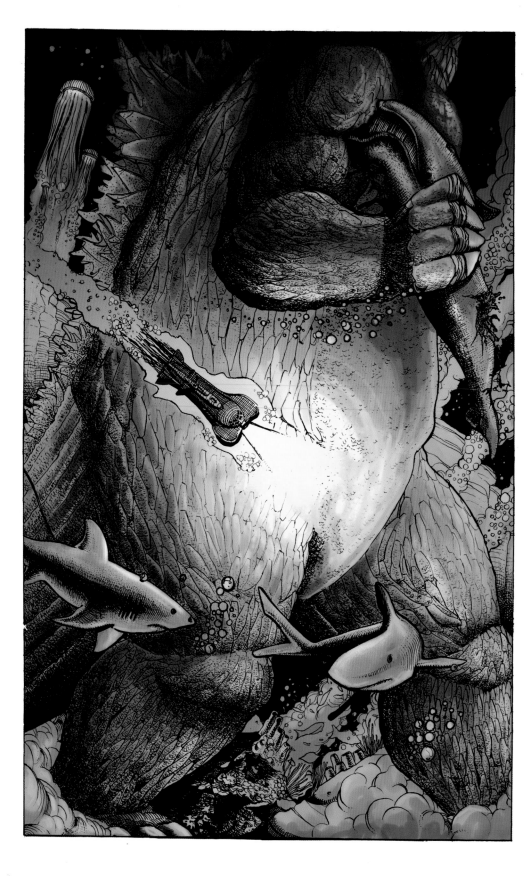

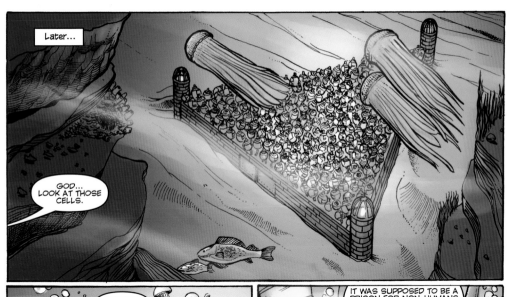

Later...

GOD... LOOK AT THOSE CELLS.

HOW DID IT GET LIKE THIS?

TAKE A GUESS.

ANOTHER OF McCARTHY'S BRIGHT IDEAS?

BINGO.

IT WAS SUPPOSED TO BE A PRISON FOR NON-HUMANS BUT ACCORDING TO THE WRITING ON THE INSIDE OF THIS CELL, APPARENTLY THEY ONLY LOCKED UP COMMIES.

Eh... people, excuse me for the catch phrase but...

Something moved over there.

QUICKLY! BEFORE HE SWALLOWS MORE WATER!

EASY, BUDDY. JUST TAKE A DEEP BREATH.

HHHHHHHH!

⦃KAFF⦄ TH-THANKS! I KNEW YOU WOULDN'T LET ME DROWN! NOT FOR JUST BEING A SUBVERSIVE WRITER!

THEY ABANDONED ME FOR SAYING THAT TROTSKY WOULD HAVE BEEN BETTER THAN STALIN! CAN YOU BELIEVE IT?

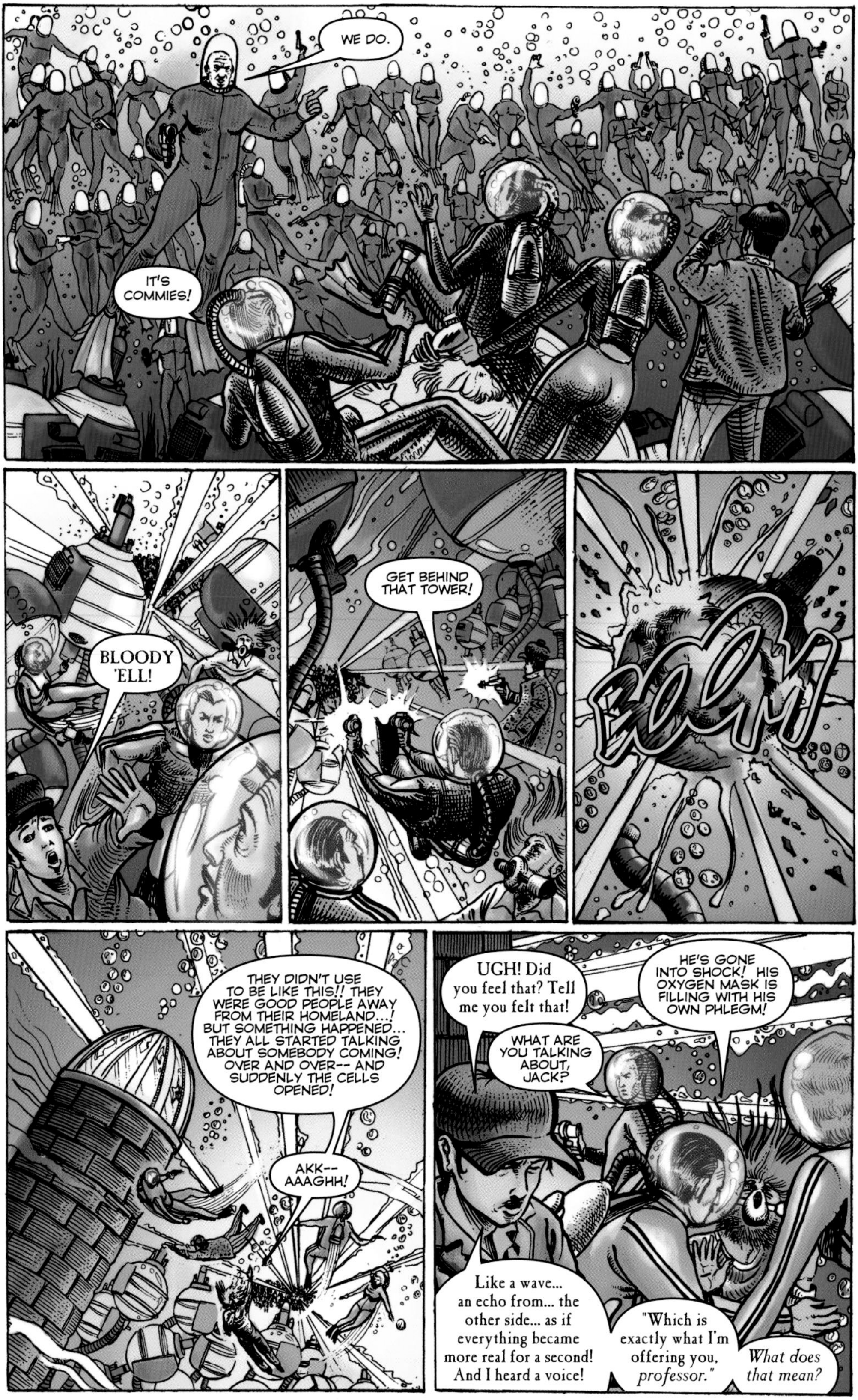
WE DO.
IT'S COMMIES!
BLOODY 'ELL!
GET BEHIND THAT TOWER!
BOOM
THEY DIDN'T USE TO BE LIKE THIS!! THEY WERE GOOD PEOPLE AWAY FROM THEIR HOMELAND...! BUT SOMETHING HAPPENED... THEY ALL STARTED TALKING ABOUT SOMEBODY COMING! OVER AND OVER-- AND SUDDENLY THE CELLS OPENED!
AKK-- AAAGHH!
UGH! Did you feel that? Tell me you felt that!
WHAT ARE YOU TALKING ABOUT, JACK?
HE'S GONE INTO SHOCK! HIS OXYGEN MASK IS FILLING WITH HIS OWN PHLEGM!
Like a wave... an echo from... the other side... as if everything became more real for a second! And I heard a voice!
"Which is exactly what I'm offering you, *professor.*"
*What does that mean?*

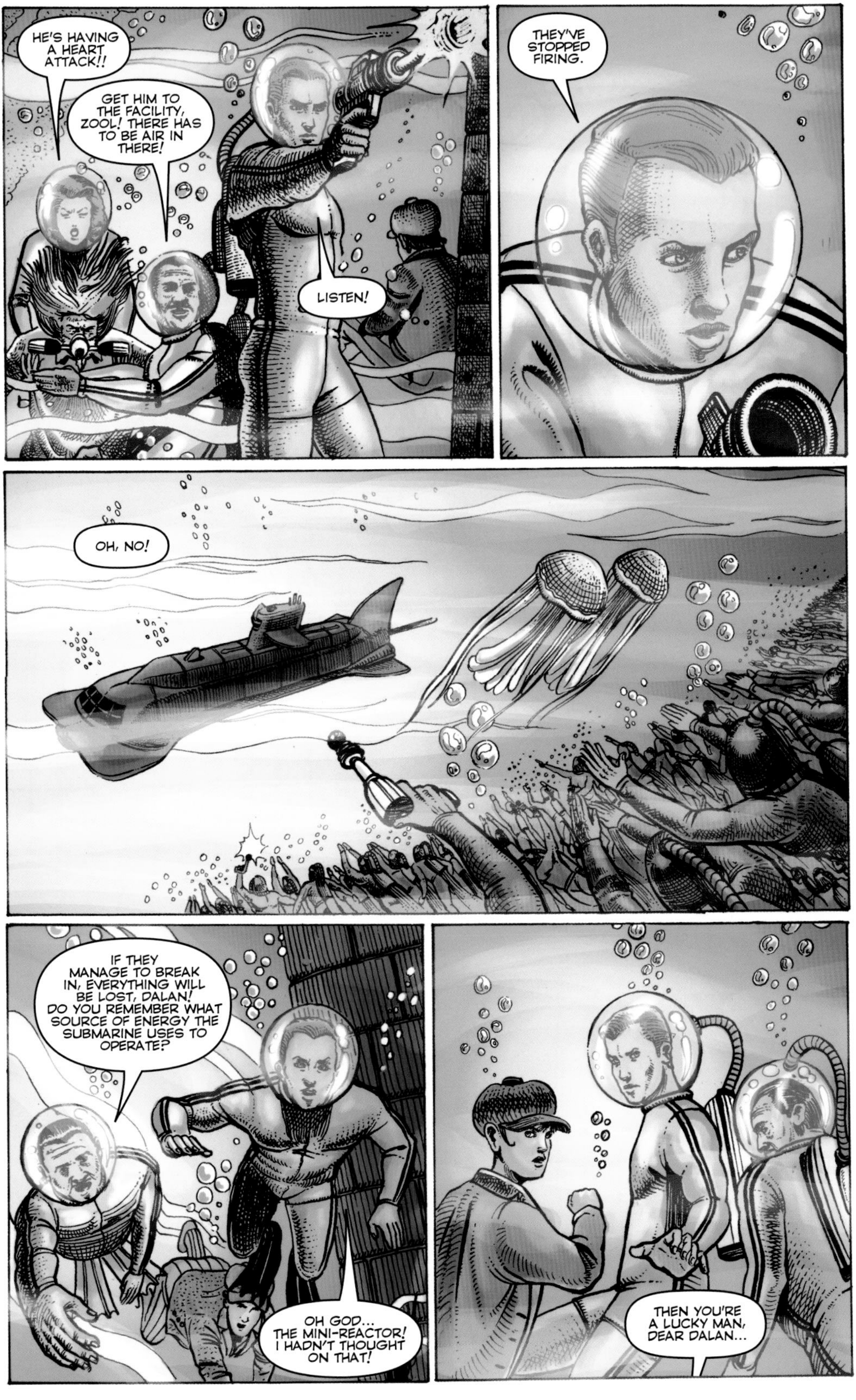
HE'S HAVING A HEART ATTACK!!
GET HIM TO THE FACILITY, ZOOL! THERE HAS TO BE AIR IN THERE!
LISTEN!
THEY'VE STOPPED FIRING.
OH, NO!
IF THEY MANAGE TO BREAK IN, EVERYTHING WILL BE LOST, DALAN! DO YOU REMEMBER WHAT SOURCE OF ENERGY THE SUBMARINE USES TO OPERATE?
OH GOD... THE MINI-REACTOR! I HADN'T THOUGHT ON THAT!
THEN YOU'RE A LUCKY MAN, DEAR DALAN...

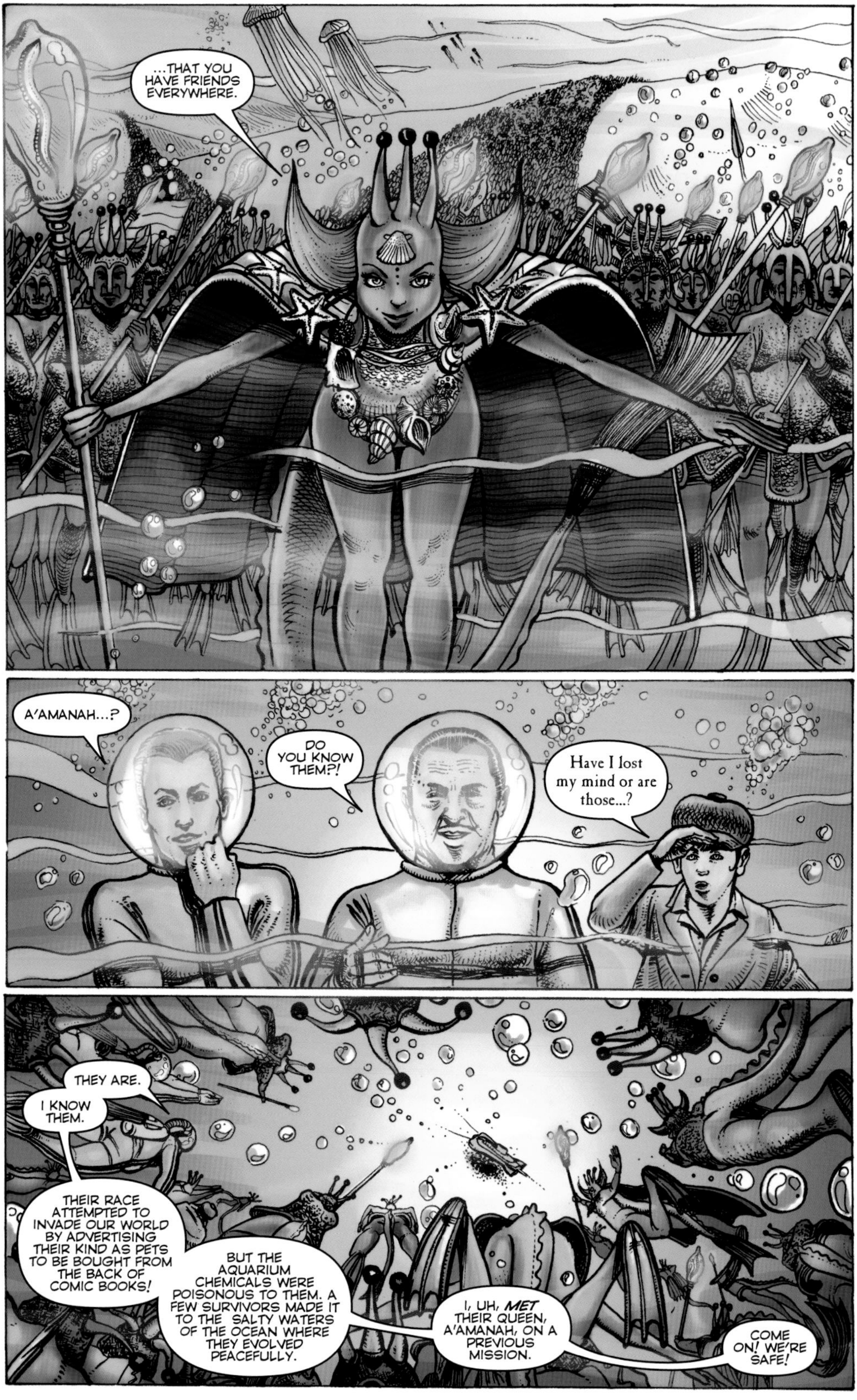
...THAT YOU HAVE FRIENDS EVERYWHERE.
A'AMANAH...?
DO YOU KNOW THEM?!
Have I lost my mind or are those...?
THEY ARE.
I KNOW THEM.
THEIR RACE ATTEMPTED TO INVADE OUR WORLD BY ADVERTISING THEIR KIND AS PETS TO BE BOUGHT FROM THE BACK OF COMIC BOOKS!
BUT THE AQUARIUM CHEMICALS WERE POISONOUS TO THEM. A FEW SURVIVORS MADE IT TO THE SALTY WATERS OF THE OCEAN WHERE THEY EVOLVED PEACEFULLY.
I, UH, *MET* THEIR QUEEN, A'AMANAH, ON A PREVIOUS MISSION.
COME ON! WE'RE SAFE!

# Then...

I DON'T KNOW HOW TO THANK YOU, A'AMANAH.

YOU DON'T NEED TO THANK ME, DARLING.

THE ONLY THING WE DID TODAY WAS SETTLE AN OLD DEBT.

OR DID YOU THINK WE'D FORGOTTEN YOUR HELP IN PREVENTING THE *INTRATERRESTRIAL* INVASION?

AND YOU MUST BE MY DARLING'S NEW *CONSORT*.

EEH... YES--I MEAN NO! ¿HEH¿ ZOOL, A'AMANAH. A'AMANAH, ZOOL.

IT'S AN HONOR, YOUR WETNESS. HAVE YOU KNOWN EACH OTHER LONG?

OH, NOT LONG ENOUGH, DARLING. BUT LET'S NOT WASTE ANY MORE TIME AND GO CELEBRATE OUR VICTORY IN MY KINGDOM. I HAVE A GOLDEN SEAWEED DRESS YOU CAN BORROW, PRECIOUS, IF YOU CAN FIT YOUR WIDE, HUMAN FRAME INTO IT...

¿HMP¿ WE APPRECIATE YOUR OFFER, HIGHNESS, BUT WE HAVE TO COMPLETE THE MISSION AND RETURN THESE POLITICAL PRISONERS TO RUSSIA. ISN'T THAT RIGHT, 'DARLING...'?

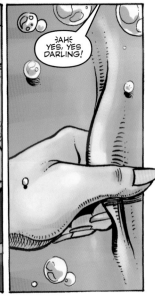

¿AH¿ YES, YES DARLING!

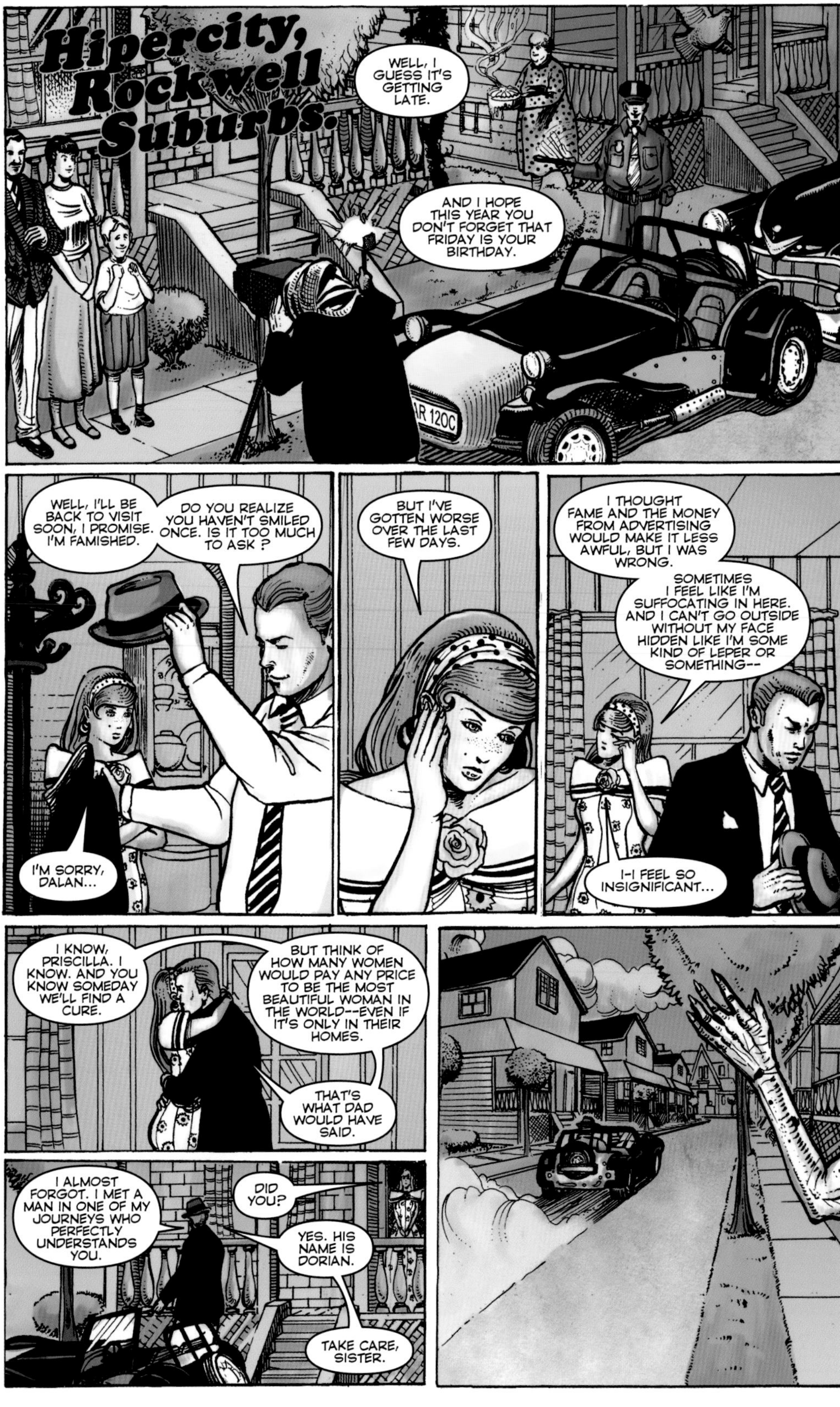
Hipercity, Rockwell Suburbs.
WELL, I GUESS IT'S GETTING LATE.
AND I HOPE THIS YEAR YOU DON'T FORGET THAT FRIDAY IS YOUR BIRTHDAY.
AR 120C
WELL, I'LL BE BACK TO VISIT SOON, I PROMISE. I'M FAMISHED.
DO YOU REALIZE YOU HAVEN'T SMILED ONCE. IS IT TOO MUCH TO ASK ?
I'M SORRY, DALAN...
BUT I'VE GOTTEN WORSE OVER THE LAST FEW DAYS.
I THOUGHT FAME AND THE MONEY FROM ADVERTISING WOULD MAKE IT LESS AWFUL, BUT I WAS WRONG.
SOMETIMES I FEEL LIKE I'M SUFFOCATING IN HERE. AND I CAN'T GO OUTSIDE WITHOUT MY FACE HIDDEN LIKE I'M SOME KIND OF LEPER OR SOMETHING--
I-I FEEL SO INSIGNIFICANT...
I KNOW, PRISCILLA. I KNOW. AND YOU KNOW SOMEDAY WE'LL FIND A CURE.
BUT THINK OF HOW MANY WOMEN WOULD PAY ANY PRICE TO BE THE MOST BEAUTIFUL WOMAN IN THE WORLD--EVEN IF IT'S ONLY IN THEIR HOMES.
THAT'S WHAT DAD WOULD HAVE SAID.
I ALMOST FORGOT. I MET A MAN IN ONE OF MY JOURNEYS WHO PERFECTLY UNDERSTANDS YOU.
DID YOU?
YES. HIS NAME IS DORIAN.
TAKE CARE, SISTER.

Allen St.

WHAT DO YOU *THINK?* THAT I WORE THE NEURONAL MULTIPLICATOR FOR SEVEN HOURS AND CAME UP WITH A *DIFFERENT* CONCLUSION?

AFTER THE SPECTACULAR FAILURE OF THE B.E.Y.O.N.D. PROJECT, MY CARREER HAS REACHED AN END, MY FRIEND.

HAVE YOU THOUGHT IT OVER, PROFESSOR?

BUT, PROFESSOR...! THE *WONDERS* YOU'VE CREATED! THE SUIT THAT MOVES THROUGH EVEN NUMBER DIMENSIONS! THE POCKET SUN! THE TRANSINFINITE NUMBERS HIVE! THE *COLOSSUS* WOULDN'T HAVE EVEN BEEN POSSIBLE WITHOUT YOUR IDEAS.

AND NONE OF THOSE THINGS HAVE MADE MY LIFE ANY BETTER, JON! I CAN'T EVEN GET YOU OUT OF THAT DAMN PERSONAL DIMENSION YOU'RE STUCK IN!

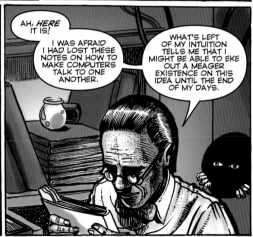

AH, *HERE* IT IS!

I WAS AFRAID I HAD LOST THESE NOTES ON HOW TO MAKE COMPUTERS TALK TO ONE ANOTHER.

WHAT'S LEFT OF MY INTUITION TELLS ME THAT I MIGHT BE ABLE TO EKE OUT A MEAGER EXISTENCE ON THIS IDEA UNTIL THE END OF MY DAYS.

‡SIGH‡ I ONLY WANTED TO GO OUT WITH ONE LAST, INGENIOUS MASTER-PLAN.

WWW.

WHICH IS *EXACTLY* WHAT I'M OFFERING YOU, PROFESSOR.

CALL ME *AGENT X*...

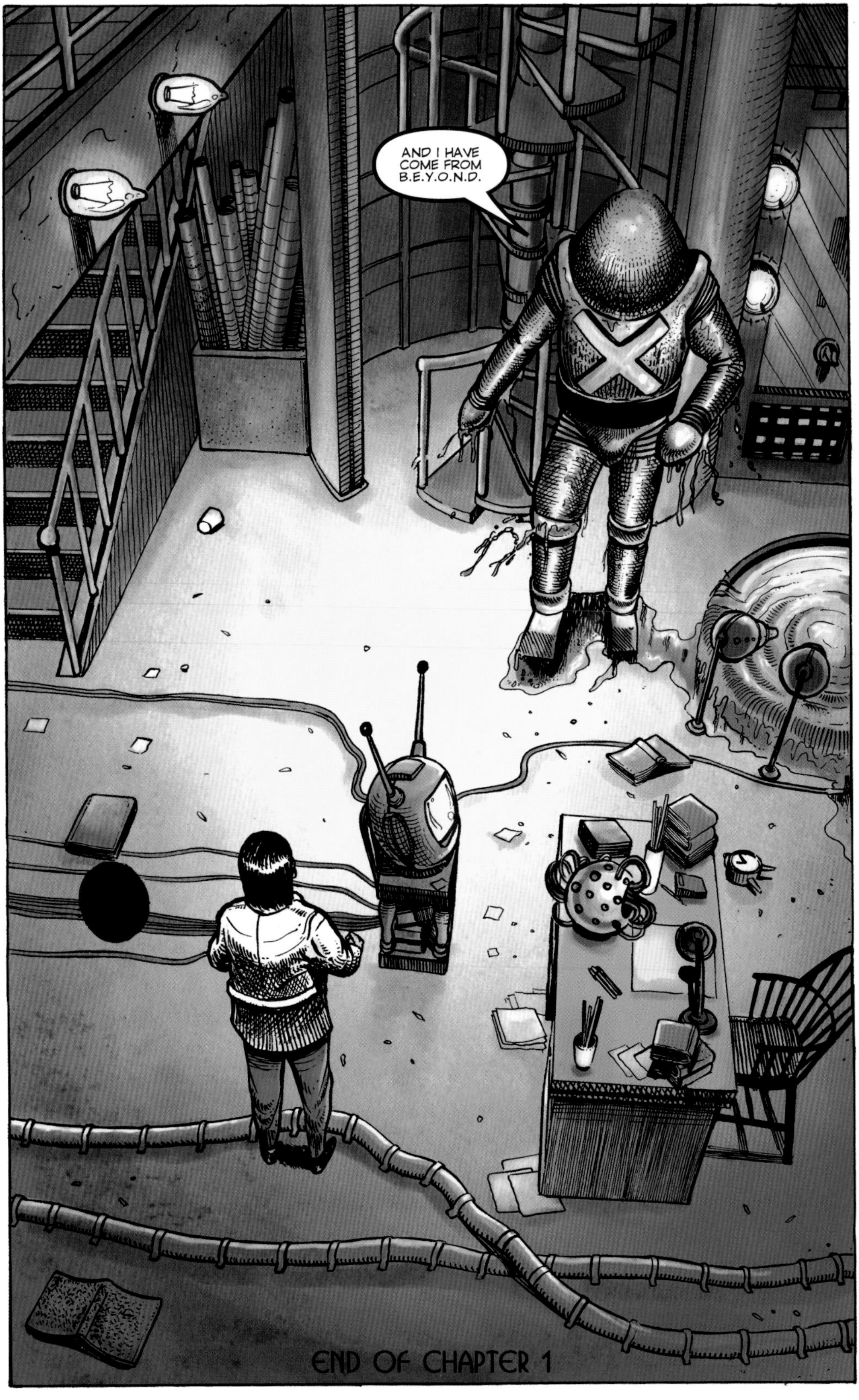
AND I HAVE COME FROM B.E.Y.O.N.D.
END OF CHAPTER 1

# CHAPTER 2
# THE MAN FROM
# B.E.Y.O.N.D.

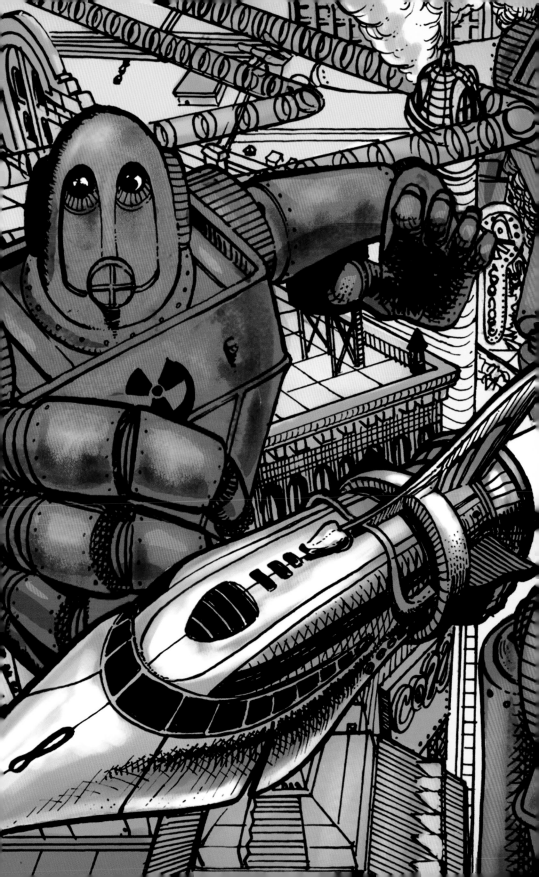

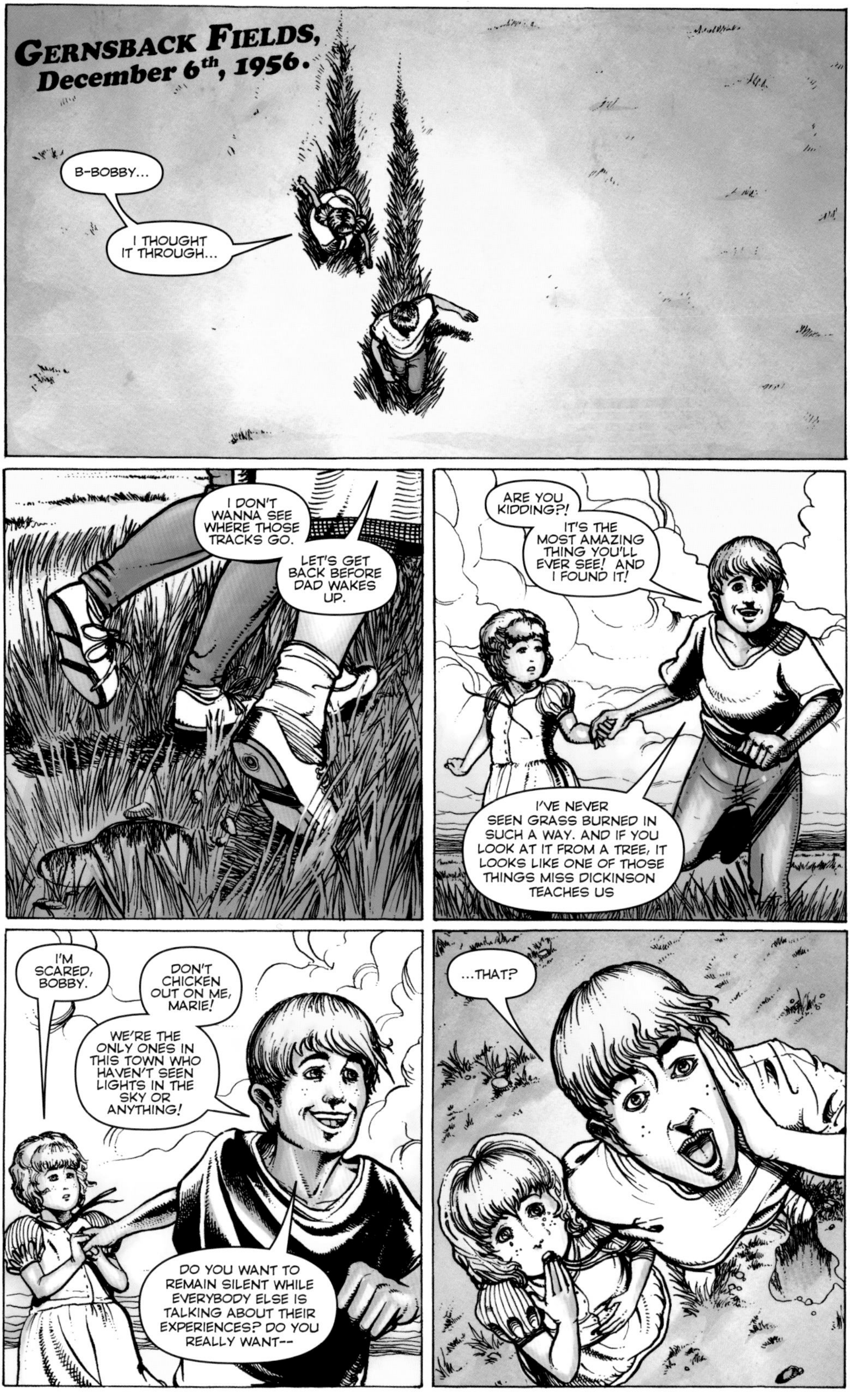
GERNSBACK FIELDS, December 6th, 1956.
B-BOBBY...
I THOUGHT IT THROUGH...
I DON'T WANNA SEE WHERE THOSE TRACKS GO.
LET'S GET BACK BEFORE DAD WAKES UP.
ARE YOU KIDDING?!
IT'S THE MOST AMAZING THING YOU'LL EVER SEE! AND I FOUND IT!
I'VE NEVER SEEN GRASS BURNED IN SUCH A WAY. AND IF YOU LOOK AT IT FROM A TREE, IT LOOKS LIKE ONE OF THOSE THINGS MISS DICKINSON TEACHES US
I'M SCARED, BOBBY.
DON'T CHICKEN OUT ON ME, MARIE!
WE'RE THE ONLY ONES IN THIS TOWN WHO HAVEN'T SEEN LIGHTS IN THE SKY OR ANYTHING!
DO YOU WANT TO REMAIN SILENT WHILE EVERYBODY ELSE IS TALKING ABOUT THEIR EXPERIENCES? DO YOU REALLY WANT--
...THAT?

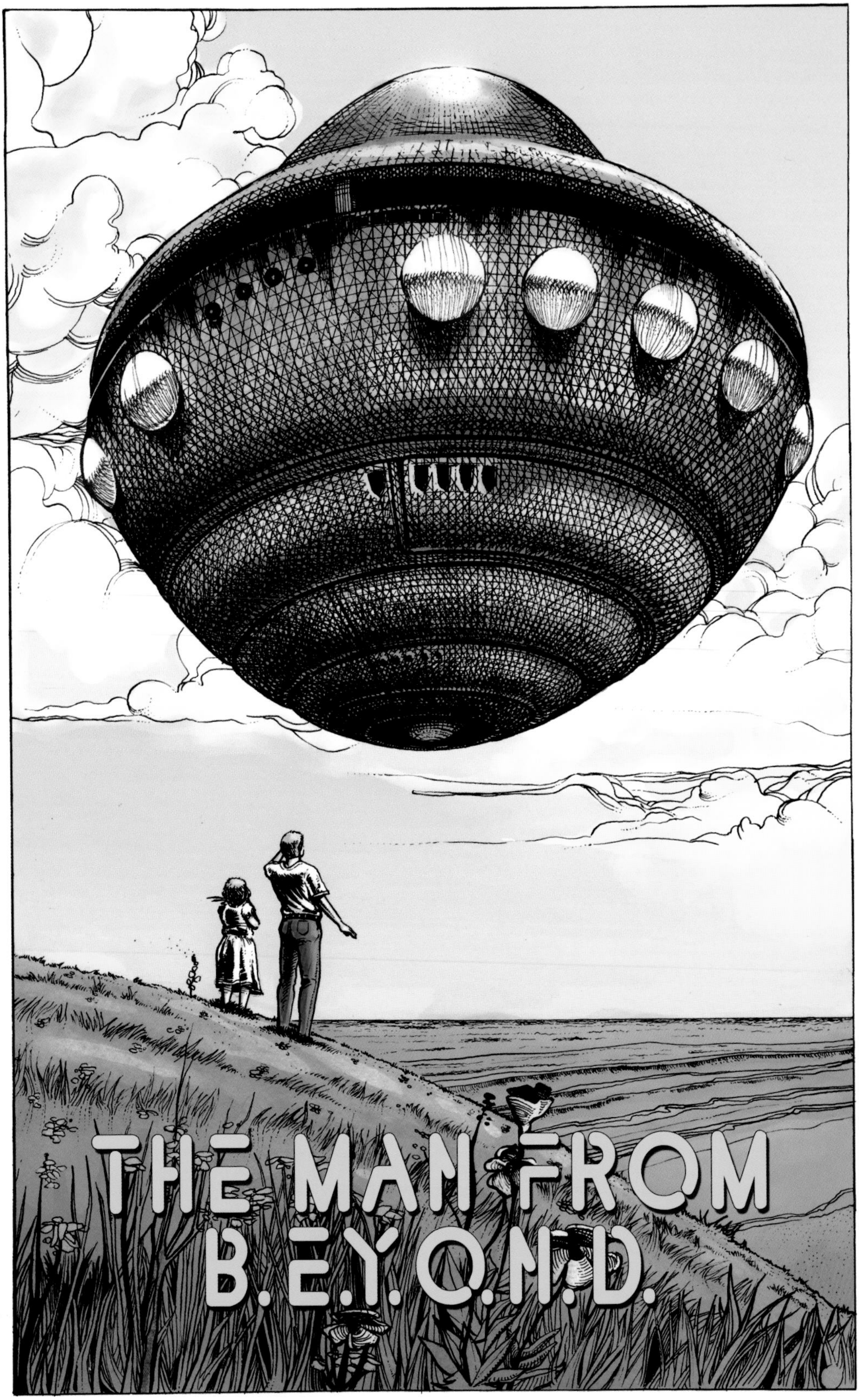
THE MAN FROM
B.E.Y.O.N.D.

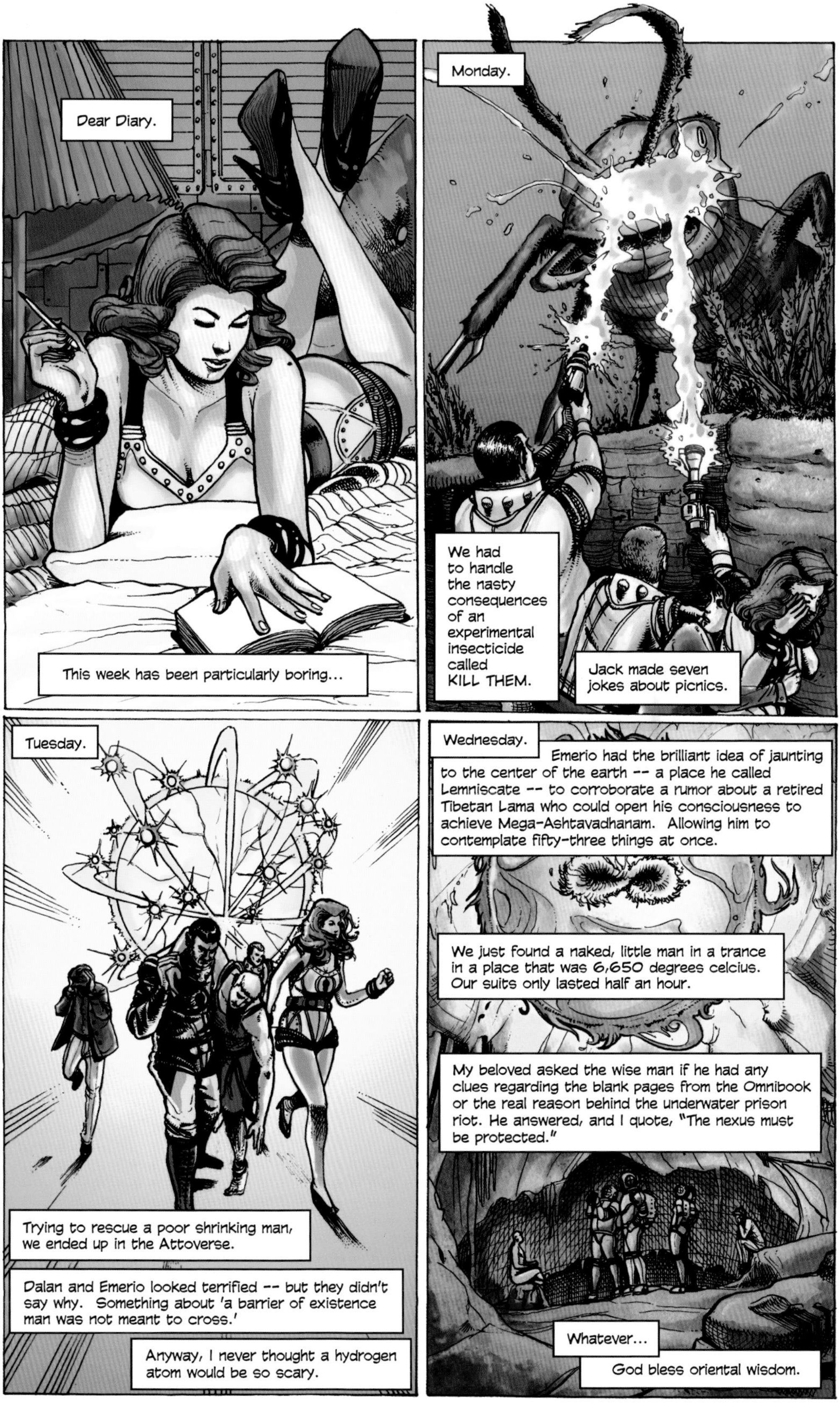
Dear Diary.
This week has been particularly boring...
Monday.
We had to handle the nasty consequences of an experimental insecticide called KILL THEM.
Jack made seven jokes about picnics.
Tuesday.
Trying to rescue a poor shrinking man, we ended up in the Attoverse.
Dalan and Emerio looked terrified -- but they didn't say why. Something about 'a barrier of existence man was not meant to cross.'
Anyway, I never thought a hydrogen atom would be so scary.
Wednesday.
Emerio had the brilliant idea of jaunting to the center of the earth -- a place he called Lemniscate -- to corroborate a rumor about a retired Tibetan Lama who could open his consciousness to achieve Mega-Ashtavadhanam. Allowing him to contemplate fifty-three things at once.
We just found a naked, little man in a trance in a place that was 6,650 degrees celcius. Our suits only lasted half an hour.
My beloved asked the wise man if he had any clues regarding the blank pages from the Omnibook or the real reason behind the underwater prison riot. He answered, and I quote, "The nexus must be protected."
Whatever...
God bless oriental wisdom.

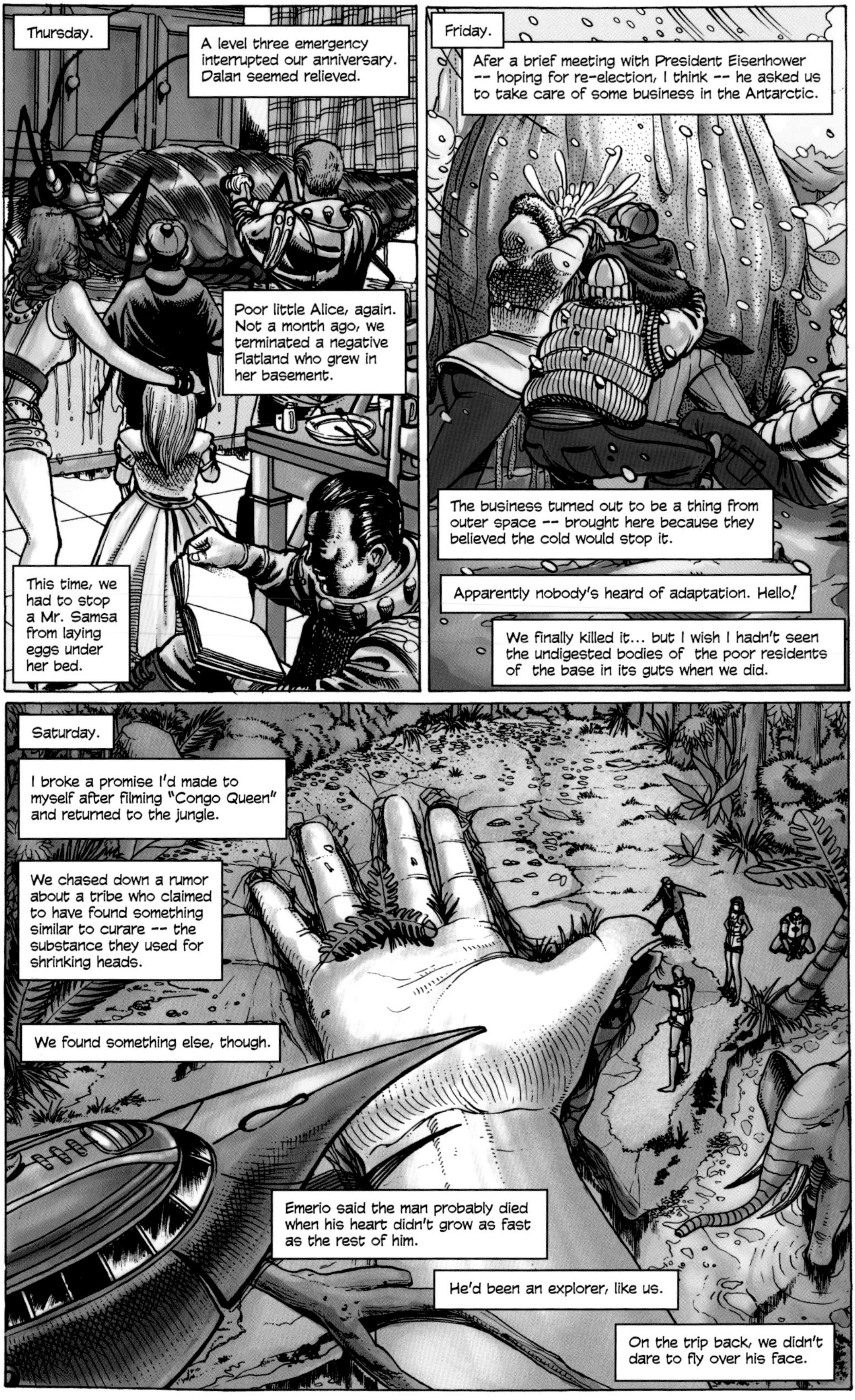
Thursday.
A level three emergency interrupted our anniversary. Dalan seemed relieved.
Poor little Alice, again. Not a month ago, we terminated a negative Flatland who grew in her basement.
This time, we had to stop a Mr. Samsa from laying eggs under her bed.
Friday.
Afer a brief meeting with President Eisenhower -- hoping for re-election, I think -- he asked us to take care of some business in the Antarctic.
The business turned out to be a thing from outer space -- brought here because they believed the cold would stop it.
Apparently nobody's heard of adaptation. Hello!
We finally killed it... but I wish I hadn't seen the undigested bodies of the poor residents of the base in its guts when we did.
Saturday.
I broke a promise I'd made to myself after filming "Congo Queen" and returned to the jungle.
We chased down a rumor about a tribe who claimed to have found something similar to curare -- the substance they used for shrinking heads.
We found something else, though.
Emerio said the man probably died when his heart didn't grow as fast as the rest of him.
He'd been an explorer, like us.
On the trip back, we didn't dare to fly over his face.

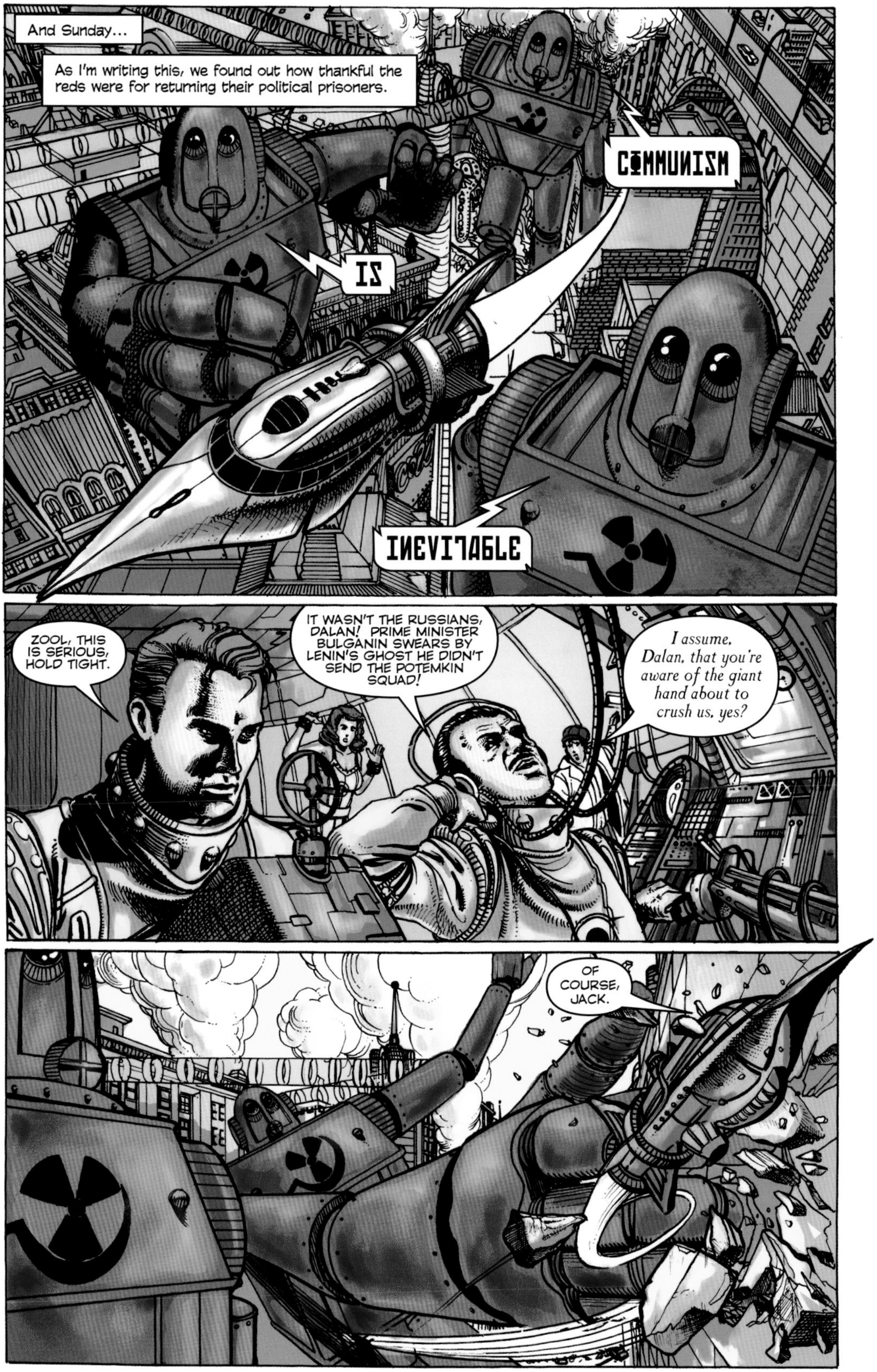
And Sunday...
As I'm writing this, we found out how thankful the reds were for returning their political prisoners.
COMMUNISM
IS
INEVITABLE
ZOOL, THIS IS SERIOUS, HOLD TIGHT.
IT WASN'T THE RUSSIANS, DALAN! PRIME MINISTER BULGANIN SWEARS BY LENIN'S GHOST HE DIDN'T SEND THE POTEMKIN SQUAD!
I assume, Dalan, that you're aware of the giant hand about to crush us, yes?
OF COURSE, JACK.

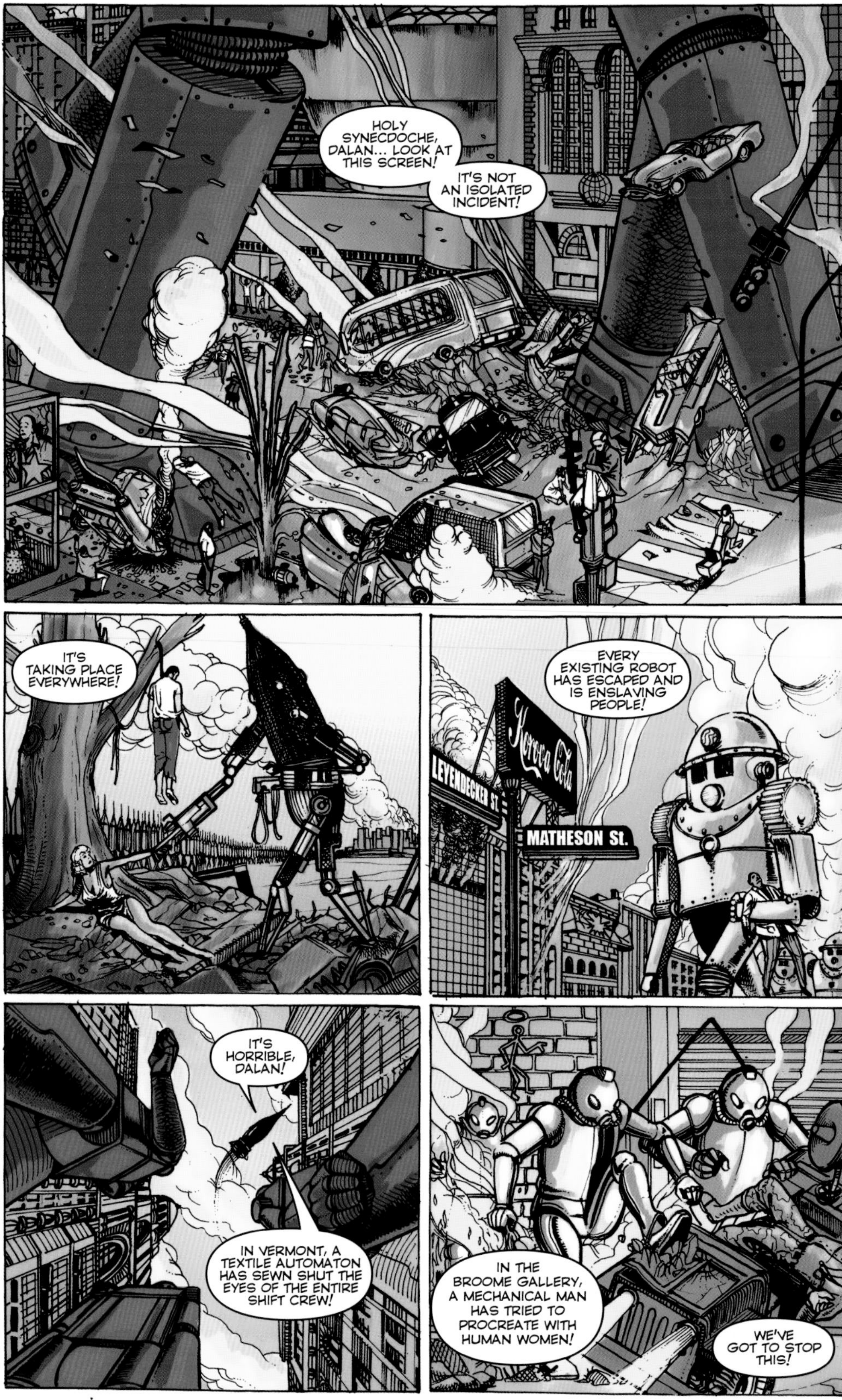
HOLY SYNECDOCHE, DALAN... LOOK AT THIS SCREEN!
IT'S NOT AN ISOLATED INCIDENT!
IT'S TAKING PLACE EVERYWHERE!
EVERY EXISTING ROBOT HAS ESCAPED AND IS ENSLAVING PEOPLE!
Korova Cola
LEYENDECKER St.
MATHESON St.
IT'S HORRIBLE, DALAN!
IN VERMONT, A TEXTILE AUTOMATON HAS SEWN SHUT THE EYES OF THE ENTIRE SHIFT CREW!
IN THE BROOME GALLERY, A MECHANICAL MAN HAS TRIED TO PROCREATE WITH HUMAN WOMEN!
WE'VE GOT TO STOP THIS!

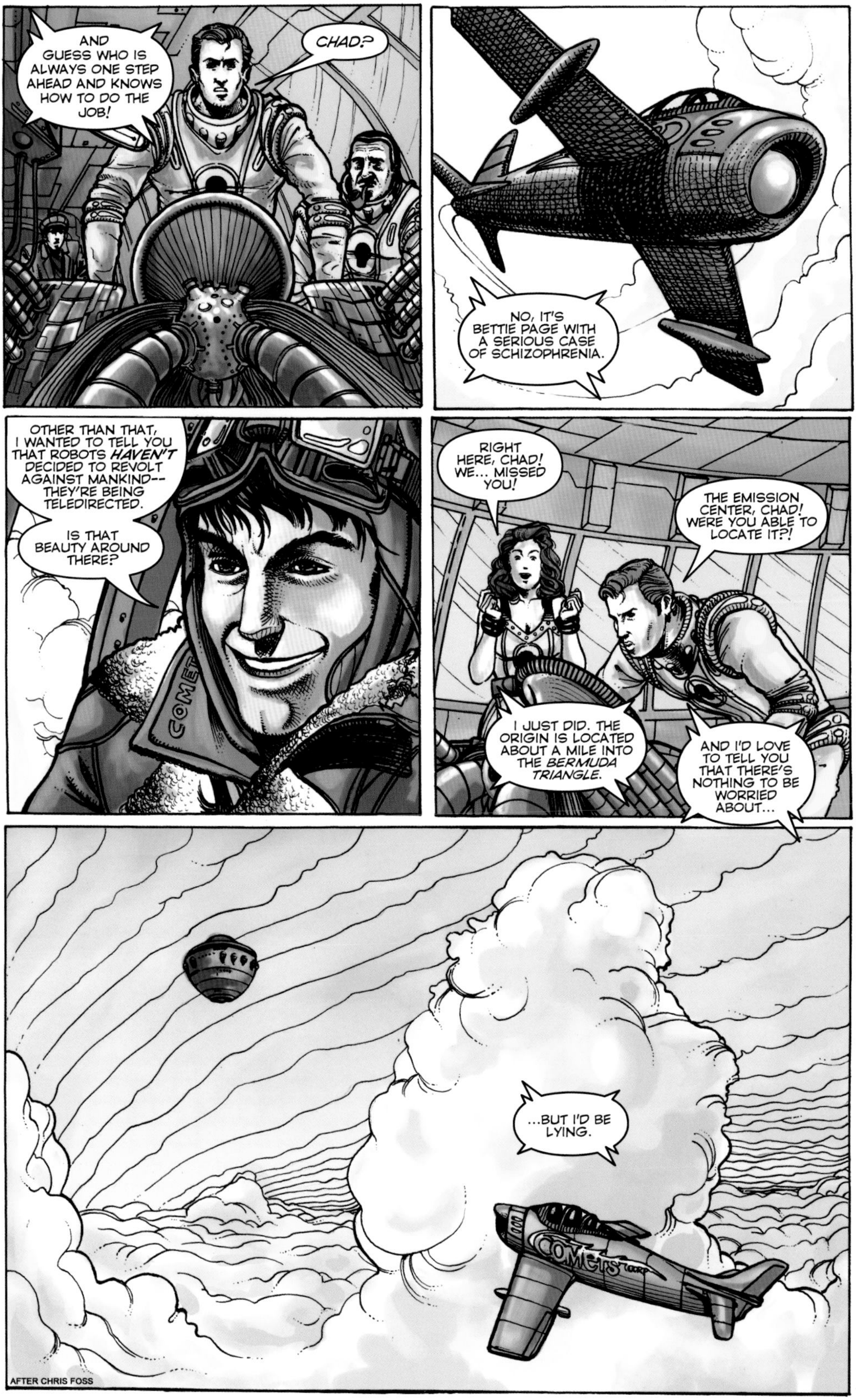
AND GUESS WHO IS ALWAYS ONE STEP AHEAD AND KNOWS HOW TO DO THE JOB!
CHAD?
NO, IT'S BETTIE PAGE WITH A SERIOUS CASE OF SCHIZOPHRENIA.
OTHER THAN THAT, I WANTED TO TELL YOU THAT ROBOTS *HAVEN'T* DECIDED TO REVOLT AGAINST MANKIND-- THEY'RE BEING TELEDIRECTED.
IS THAT BEAUTY AROUND THERE?
COMET
RIGHT HERE, CHAD! WE... MISSED YOU!
THE EMISSION CENTER, CHAD! WERE YOU ABLE TO LOCATE IT?!
I JUST DID. THE ORIGIN IS LOCATED ABOUT A MILE INTO THE *BERMUDA TRIANGLE*.
AND I'D LOVE TO TELL YOU THAT THERE'S NOTHING TO BE WORRIED ABOUT...
...BUT I'D BE LYING.
COMETS
AFTER CHRIS FOSS

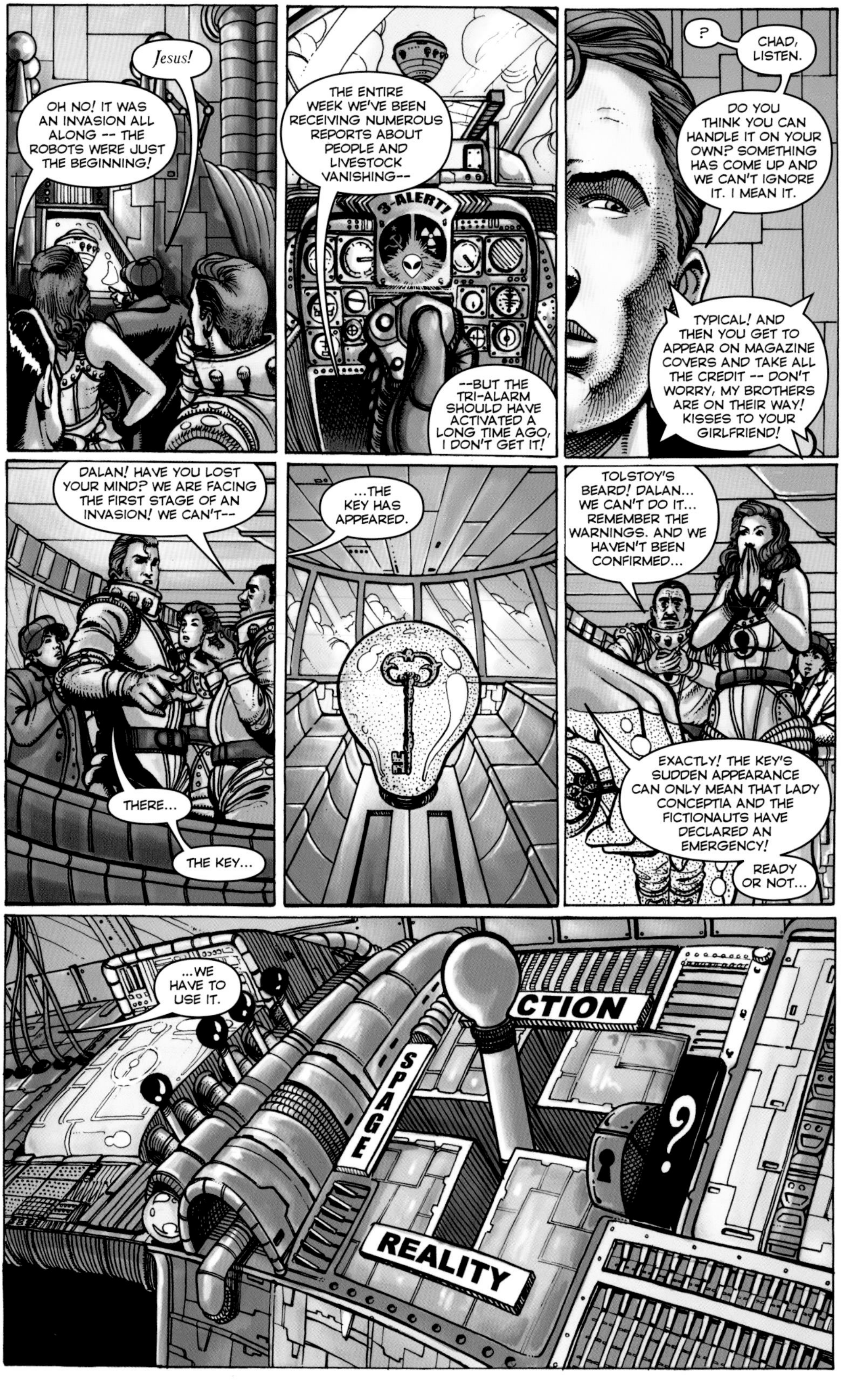
OH NO! IT WAS AN INVASION ALL ALONG -- THE ROBOTS WERE JUST THE BEGINNING!
Jesus!
THE ENTIRE WEEK WE'VE BEEN RECEIVING NUMEROUS REPORTS ABOUT PEOPLE AND LIVESTOCK VANISHING--
3-ALERT!
--BUT THE TRI-ALARM SHOULD HAVE ACTIVATED A LONG TIME AGO, I DON'T GET IT!
?
CHAD, LISTEN.
DO YOU THINK YOU CAN HANDLE IT ON YOUR OWN? SOMETHING HAS COME UP AND WE CAN'T IGNORE IT. I MEAN IT.
TYPICAL! AND THEN YOU GET TO APPEAR ON MAGAZINE COVERS AND TAKE ALL THE CREDIT -- DON'T WORRY, MY BROTHERS ARE ON THEIR WAY! KISSES TO YOUR GIRLFRIEND!
DALAN! HAVE YOU LOST YOUR MIND? WE ARE FACING THE FIRST STAGE OF AN INVASION! WE CAN'T--
THERE...
THE KEY...
...THE KEY HAS APPEARED.
TOLSTOY'S BEARD! DALAN... WE CAN'T DO IT... REMEMBER THE WARNINGS. AND WE HAVEN'T BEEN CONFIRMED...
EXACTLY! THE KEY'S SUDDEN APPEARANCE CAN ONLY MEAN THAT LADY CONCEPTIA AND THE FICTIONAUTS HAVE DECLARED AN EMERGENCY!
READY OR NOT...
...WE HAVE TO USE IT.
CTION
SPACE
REALITY
?

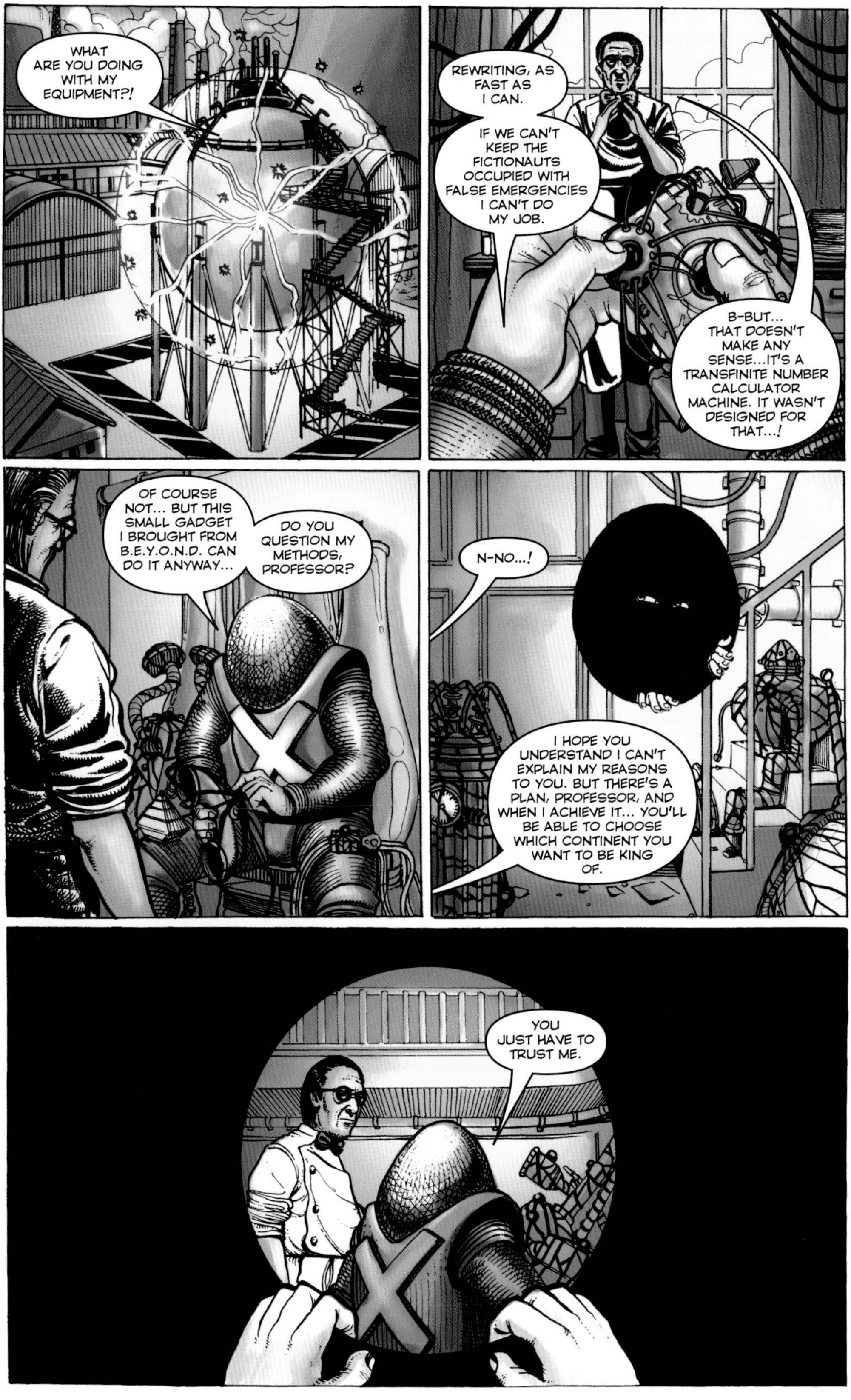
WHAT ARE YOU DOING WITH MY EQUIPMENT?!
REWRITING, AS FAST AS I CAN.
IF WE CAN'T KEEP THE FICTIONAUTS OCCUPIED WITH FALSE EMERGENCIES I CAN'T DO MY JOB.
B-BUT... THAT DOESN'T MAKE ANY SENSE...IT'S A TRANSFINITE NUMBER CALCULATOR MACHINE. IT WASN'T DESIGNED FOR THAT...!
OF COURSE NOT... BUT THIS SMALL GADGET I BROUGHT FROM B.E.Y.O.N.D. CAN DO IT ANYWAY...
DO YOU QUESTION MY METHODS, PROFESSOR?
N-NO...!
I HOPE YOU UNDERSTAND I CAN'T EXPLAIN MY REASONS TO YOU. BUT THERE'S A PLAN, PROFESSOR, AND WHEN I ACHIEVE IT... YOU'LL BE ABLE TO CHOOSE WHICH CONTINENT YOU WANT TO BE KING OF.
YOU JUST HAVE TO TRUST ME.

THE FICTIONAUTS *DON'T* HAVE A STATUE OF YOU IN THEIR GALLERY OF VILLAINS, DID YOU KNOW THAT?

THAT'S... IMPOSSIBLE! I HAVE BEEN THE ONE WHO MOST...

BUT THAT'S THE WAY IT IS. THEY HAVE THE *MULTI-MONSTER,* THE *ATMOSPHERE MAN, TRIPLO.* THERE'S EVEN ONE OF *CELULOIDO.*

I DON'T BELIEVE IT! THOSE BASTARDS!

THOSE BASTARDS CAN BE YOUR SLAVES IF YOU CONTINUE HELPING ME, DON'T YOU REALIZE THAT?

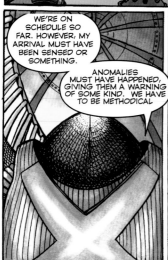

WE'RE ON SCHEDULE SO FAR. HOWEVER, MY ARRIVAL MUST HAVE BEEN SENSED OR SOMETHING.

ANOMALIES MUST HAVE HAPPENED, GIVING THEM A WARNING OF SOME KIND. WE HAVE TO BE METHODICAL

LUCKILY, WHAT I NEED NEXT IS RIGHT HERE IN THIS PLACE.

T-THAT DOOR... ONLY I CAN...

HERE.

IT'S HERE...

SOMEWHERE AMONG THIS OTHER STUFF.

11
10

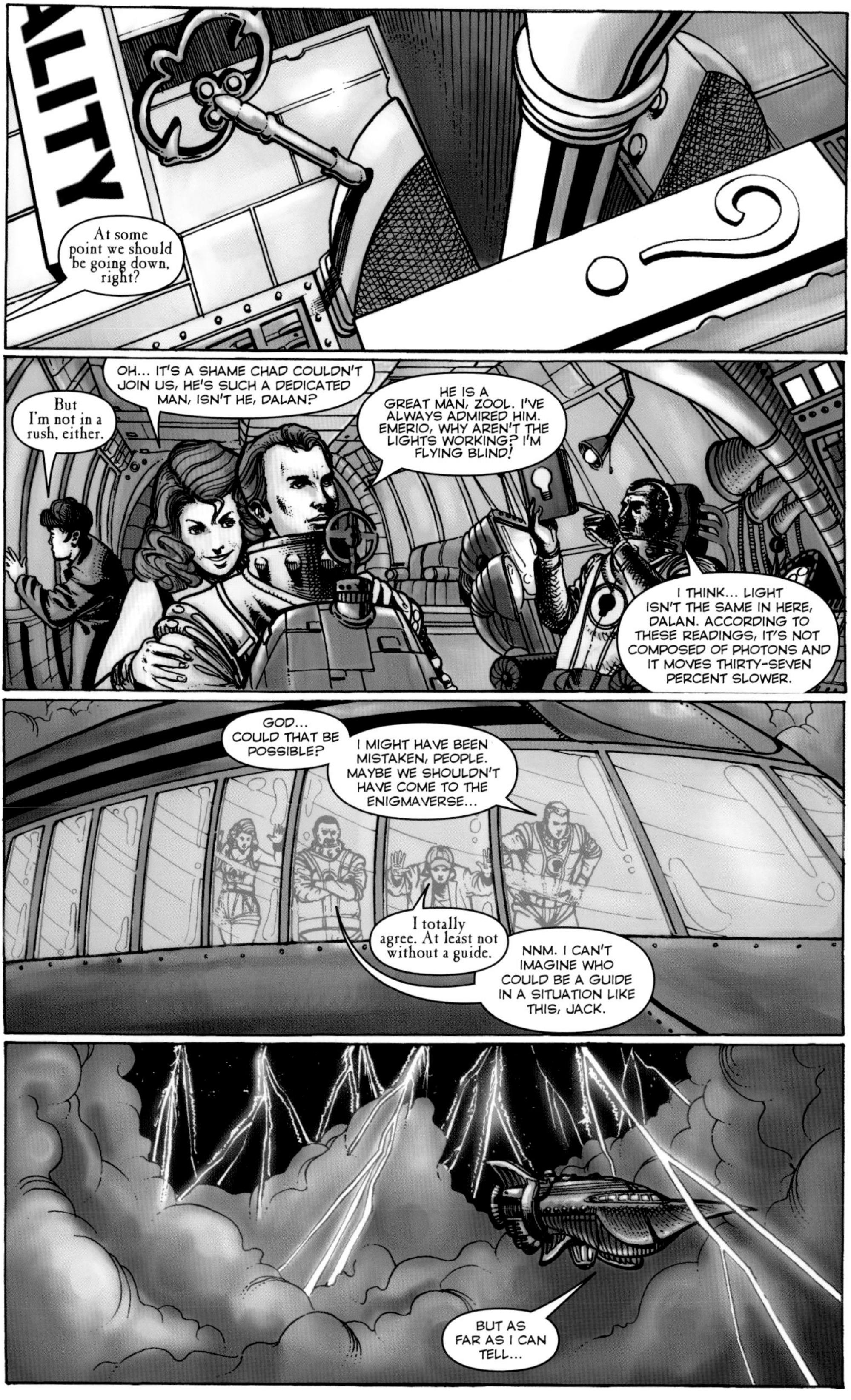
ALITY
At some point we should be going down, right?
But I'm not in a rush, either.
OH... IT'S A SHAME CHAD COULDN'T JOIN US, HE'S SUCH A DEDICATED MAN, ISN'T HE, DALAN?
HE IS A GREAT MAN, ZOOL. I'VE ALWAYS ADMIRED HIM. EMERIO, WHY AREN'T THE LIGHTS WORKING? I'M FLYING BLIND!
I THINK... LIGHT ISN'T THE SAME IN HERE, DALAN. ACCORDING TO THESE READINGS, IT'S NOT COMPOSED OF PHOTONS AND IT MOVES THIRTY-SEVEN PERCENT SLOWER.
GOD... COULD THAT BE POSSIBLE?
I MIGHT HAVE BEEN MISTAKEN, PEOPLE. MAYBE WE SHOULDN'T HAVE COME TO THE ENIGMAVERSE...
I totally agree. At least not without a guide.
NNM. I CAN'T IMAGINE WHO COULD BE A GUIDE IN A SITUATION LIKE THIS, JACK.
BUT AS FAR AS I CAN TELL...

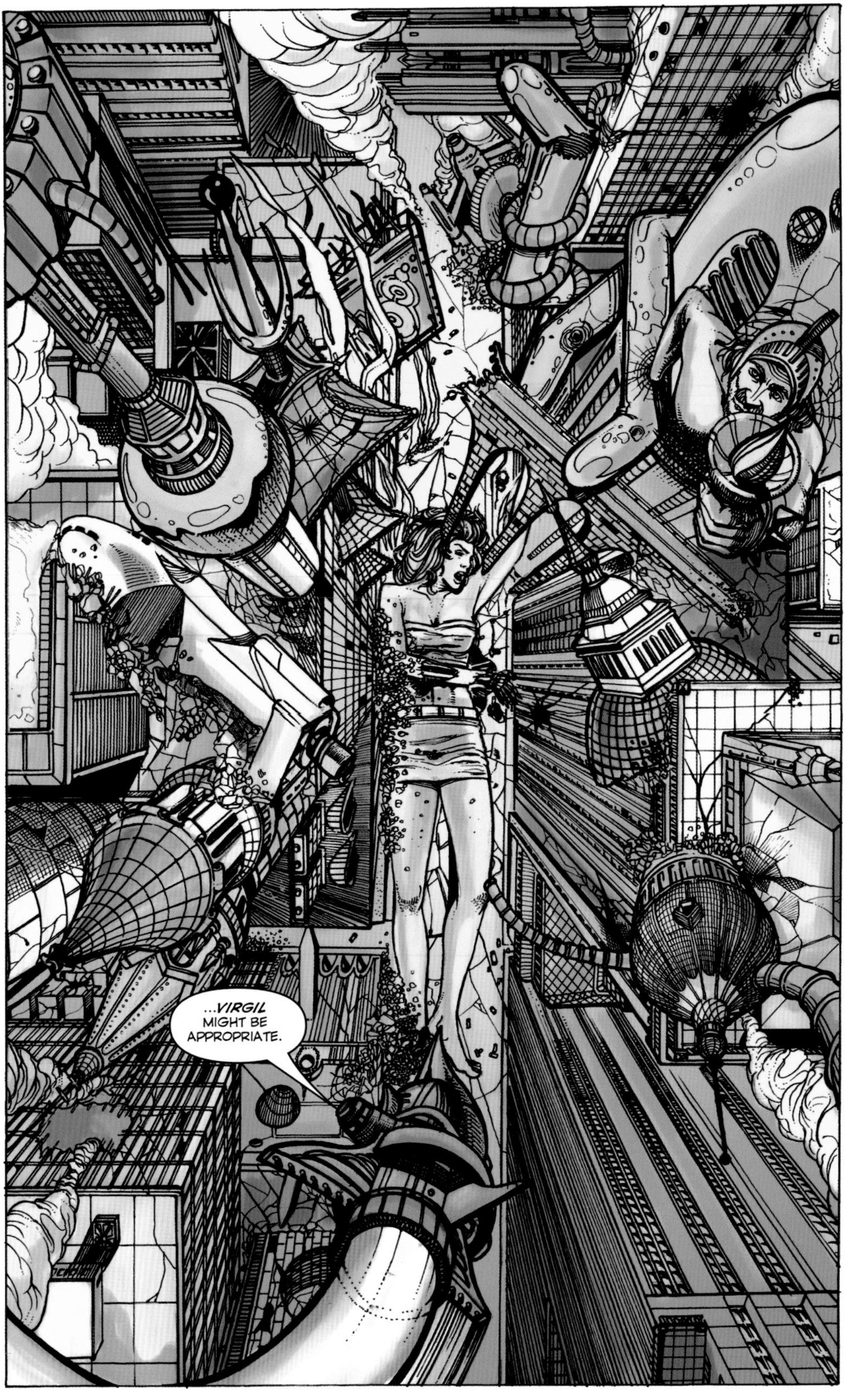
...VIRGIL MIGHT BE APPROPRIATE.

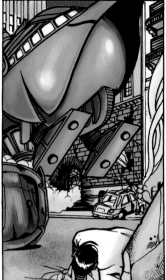
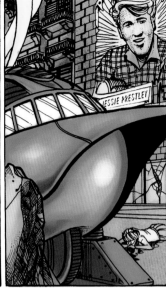

THIS IS SO CREEPY, DALAN! IS THIS ANOTHER ONE OF THOSE CLICHE ALTERNATIVE POSTNUCLEAR FUTURES?!

SOMETHING TELLS ME IT'S NOT.

THIS CAN'T BE THE FUTURE, HONEY.

I'll bet my first row seat to the Buddy Holly show that this could only have been done by Doctor Ontologic!

OR WORSE, JACK.

YOU MUST BE EXPERIENCING THE SAME DISTURBING FEELING THAT EVERYTHING LOOKS LIKE A SICK VERSION OF OUR REALITY.

YOU'RE RIGHT, PROFESSOR! BUT IN THAT CASE... WHY WEREN'T WE TOLD? WHY CALL IT THE ENIGMAVERSE?!

I'M SURE THERE'S AN EXPLANATION, DALAN. BUT I'M NOT SURE WHAT IT IS...

...OR IF WE'RE EVEN MEANT TO KNOW ABOUT IT.

FOR CRYING OUT LOUD! WHY DOES THE AIR SMELL LIKE THAT? IT'S MAKING ME DIZZY. ISN'T IT AFFECTING YOU, JACK?!

Y-yeah... I was about to say the same thing!

OH GOD, LOOK!

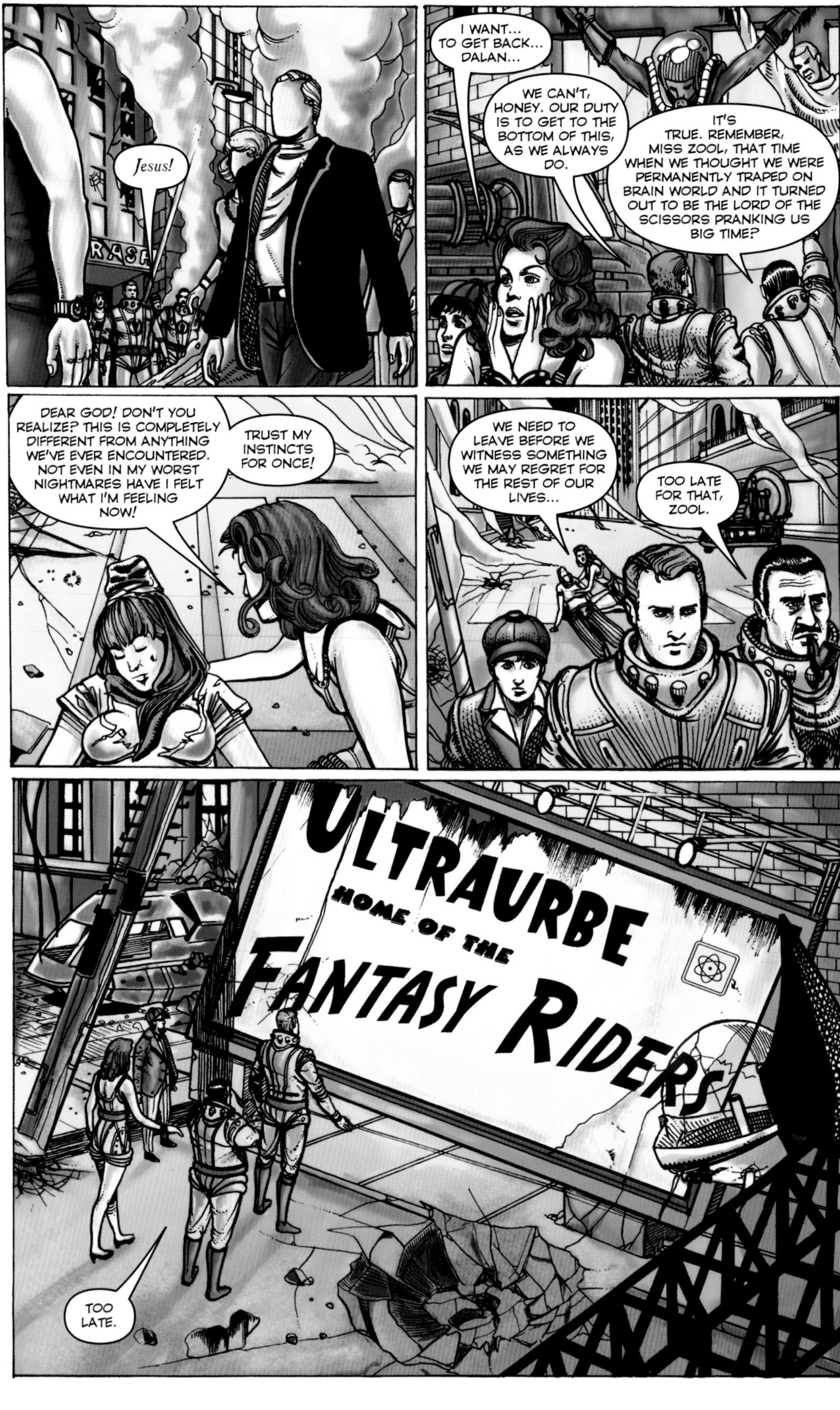
Jesus!
RASA
I WANT... TO GET BACK... DALAN...
WE CAN'T, HONEY. OUR DUTY IS TO GET TO THE BOTTOM OF THIS, AS WE ALWAYS DO.
IT'S TRUE. REMEMBER, MISS ZOOL, THAT TIME WHEN WE THOUGHT WE WERE PERMANENTLY TRAPED ON BRAIN WORLD AND IT TURNED OUT TO BE THE LORD OF THE SCISSORS PRANKING US BIG TIME?
DEAR GOD! DON'T YOU REALIZE? THIS IS COMPLETELY DIFFERENT FROM ANYTHING WE'VE EVER ENCOUNTERED. NOT EVEN IN MY WORST NIGHTMARES HAVE I FELT WHAT I'M FEELING NOW!
TRUST MY INSTINCTS FOR ONCE!
WE NEED TO LEAVE BEFORE WE WITNESS SOMETHING WE MAY REGRET FOR THE REST OF OUR LIVES...
TOO LATE FOR THAT, ZOOL.
ULTRAURBE
HOME OF THE
FANTASY RIDERS
TOO LATE.

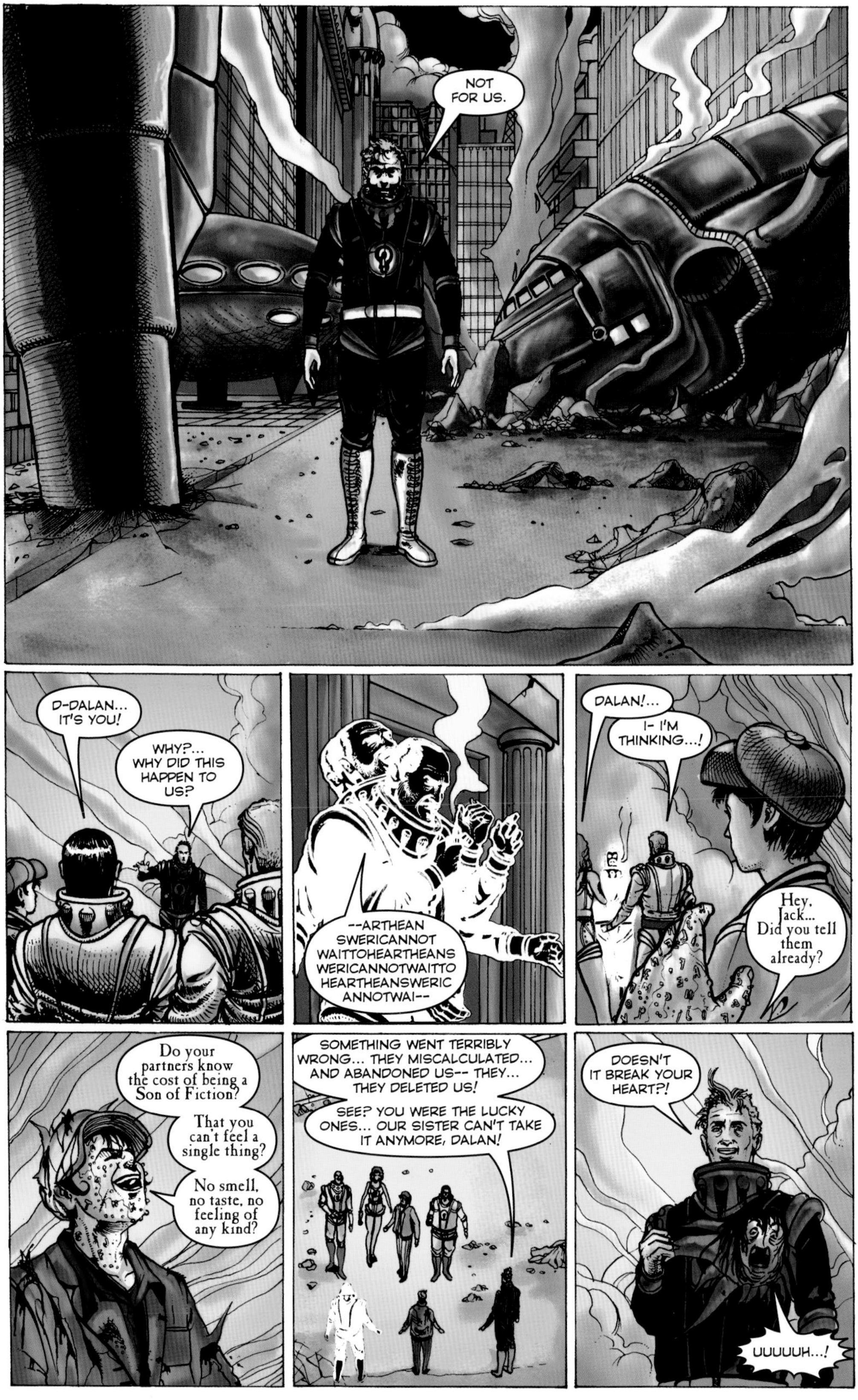
NOT FOR US.
D-DALAN... IT'S YOU!
WHY?... WHY DID THIS HAPPEN TO US?
--ARTHEAN SWERICANNOT WAITTOHEARTHEANS WERICANNOTWAITTO HEARTHEANSWERIC ANNOTWAI--
DALAN!...
I- I'M THINKING...!
Hey, Jack... Did you tell them already?
Do your partners know the cost of being a Son of Fiction?
That you can't feel a single thing?
No smell, no taste, no feeling of any kind?
SOMETHING WENT TERRIBLY WRONG... THEY MISCALCULATED... AND ABANDONED US-- THEY... THEY DELETED US!
SEE? YOU WERE THE LUCKY ONES... OUR SISTER CAN'T TAKE IT ANYMORE, DALAN!
DOESN'T IT BREAK YOUR HEART?!
UUUUUH...!

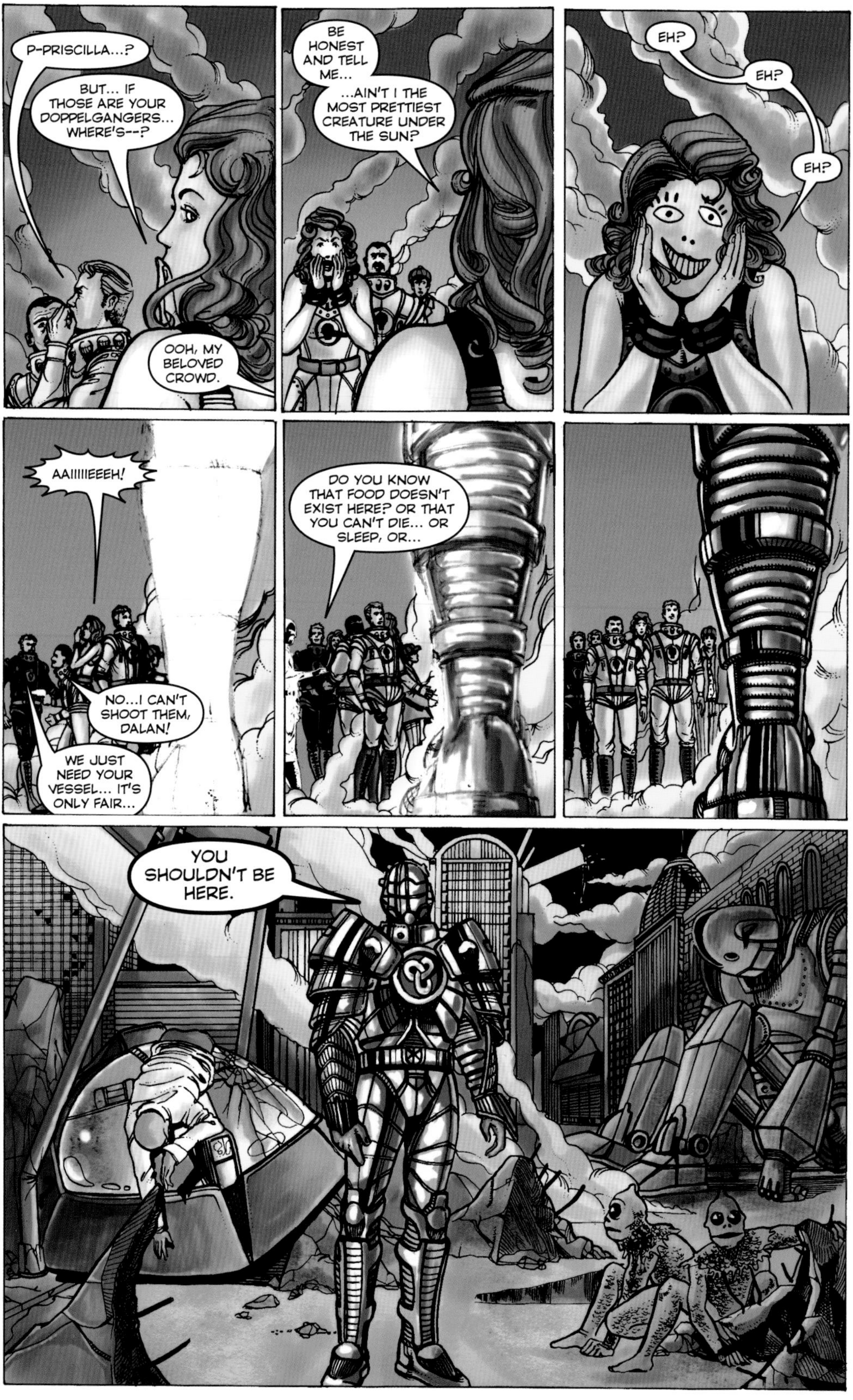
P-PRISCILLA...?
BUT... IF THOSE ARE YOUR DOPPELGANGERS... WHERE'S--?
OOH, MY BELOVED CROWD.
BE HONEST AND TELL ME...
...AIN'T I THE MOST PRETTIEST CREATURE UNDER THE SUN?
EH?
EH?
EH?
AAIIIIIEEEH!
NO...I CAN'T SHOOT THEM, DALAN!
WE JUST NEED YOUR VESSEL... IT'S ONLY FAIR...
DO YOU KNOW THAT FOOD DOESN'T EXIST HERE? OR THAT YOU CAN'T DIE... OR SLEEP, OR...
YOU SHOULDN'T BE HERE.

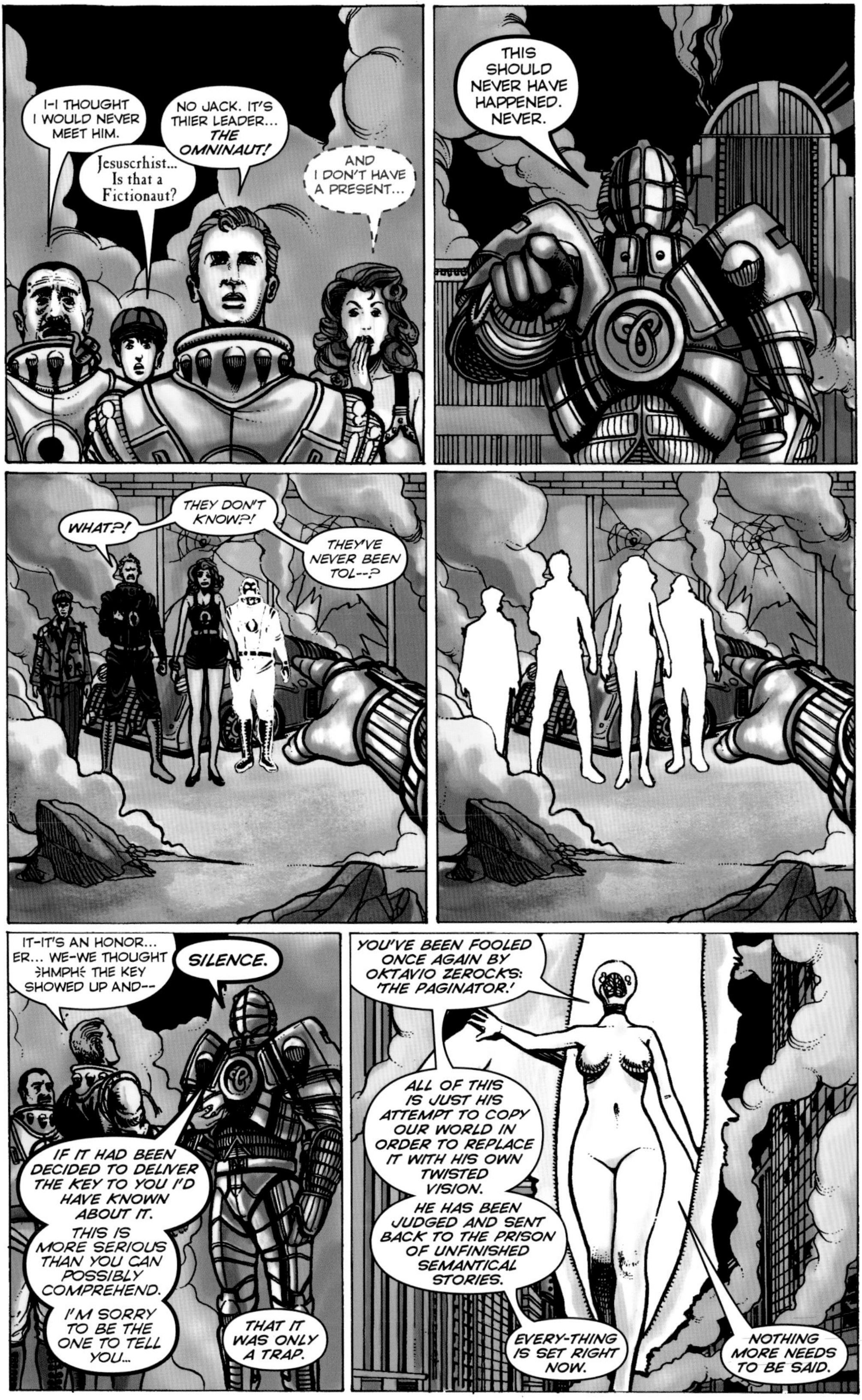
I-I THOUGHT I WOULD NEVER MEET HIM.
Jesuscrhist... Is that a Fictionaut?
NO JACK. IT'S THIER LEADER... THE OMNINAUT!
AND I DON'T HAVE A PRESENT...
THIS SHOULD NEVER HAVE HAPPENED. NEVER.
WHAT?!
THEY DON'T KNOW?!
THEY'VE NEVER BEEN TOL--?
IT-IT'S AN HONOR... ER... WE-WE THOUGHT HMPH THE KEY SHOWED UP AND--
SILENCE.
IF IT HAD BEEN DECIDED TO DELIVER THE KEY TO YOU I'D HAVE KNOWN ABOUT IT.
THIS IS MORE SERIOUS THAN YOU CAN POSSIBLY COMPREHEND.
I'M SORRY TO BE THE ONE TO TELL YOU...
THAT IT WAS ONLY A TRAP.
YOU'VE BEEN FOOLED ONCE AGAIN BY OKTAVIO ZEROCKS: 'THE PAGINATOR.'
ALL OF THIS IS JUST HIS ATTEMPT TO COPY OUR WORLD IN ORDER TO REPLACE IT WITH HIS OWN TWISTED VISION.
HE HAS BEEN JUDGED AND SENT BACK TO THE PRISON OF UNFINISHED SEMANTICAL STORIES.
EVERY-THING IS SET RIGHT NOW.
NOTHING MORE NEEDS TO BE SAID.

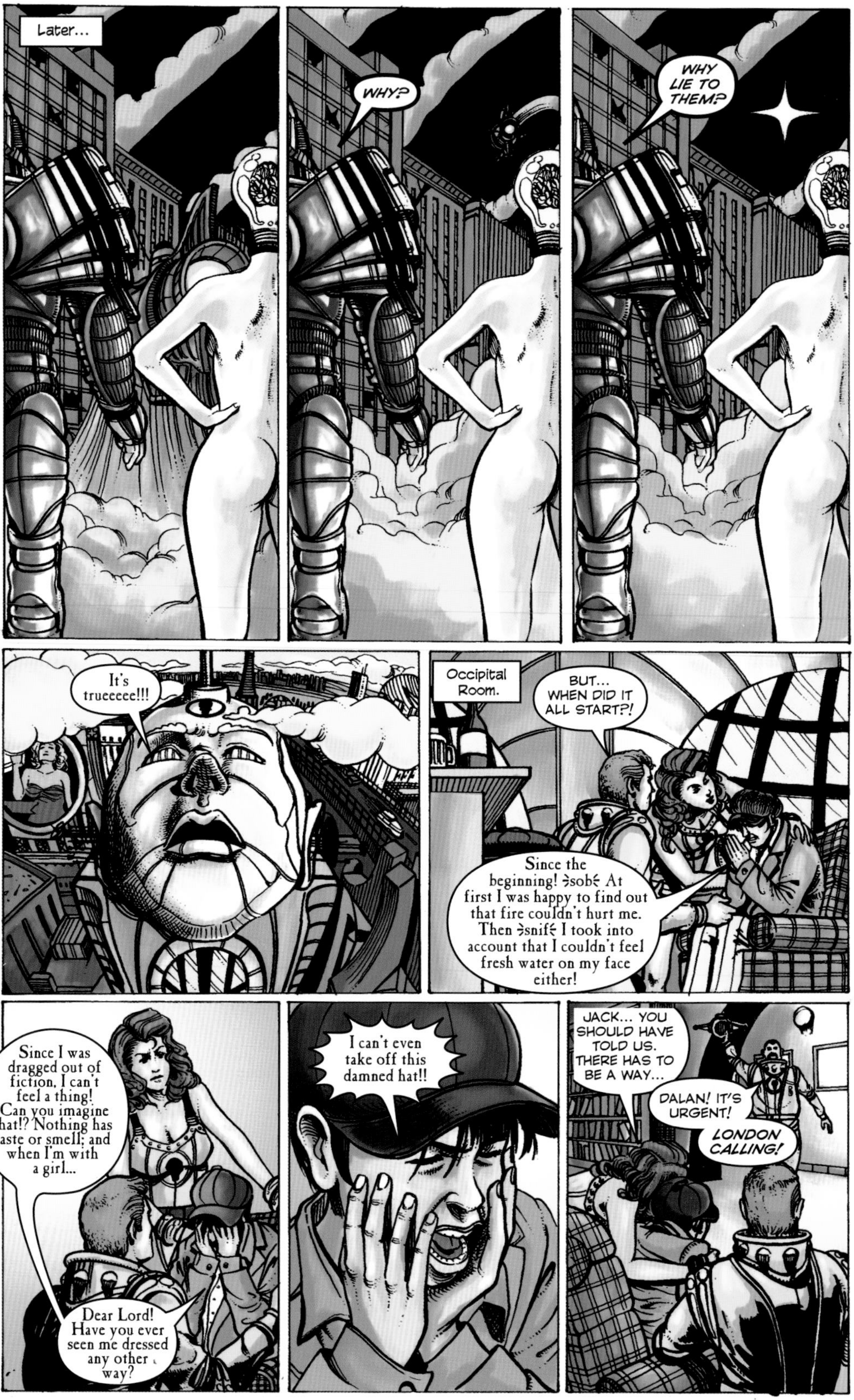

Later...
WHY?
WHY LIE TO THEM?
It's trueeeee!!!
Occipital Room.
BUT... WHEN DID IT ALL START?!
Since the beginning! ⊰sob⊱ At first I was happy to find out that fire couldn't hurt me. Then ⊰snif⊱ I took into account that I couldn't feel fresh water on my face either!
Since I was dragged out of fiction, I can't feel a thing! Can you imagine that!? Nothing has taste or smell; and when I'm with a girl...
Dear Lord! Have you ever seen me dressed any other way?
I can't even take off this damned hat!!
JACK... YOU SHOULD HAVE TOLD US. THERE HAS TO BE A WAY...
DALAN! IT'S URGENT!
LONDON CALLING!

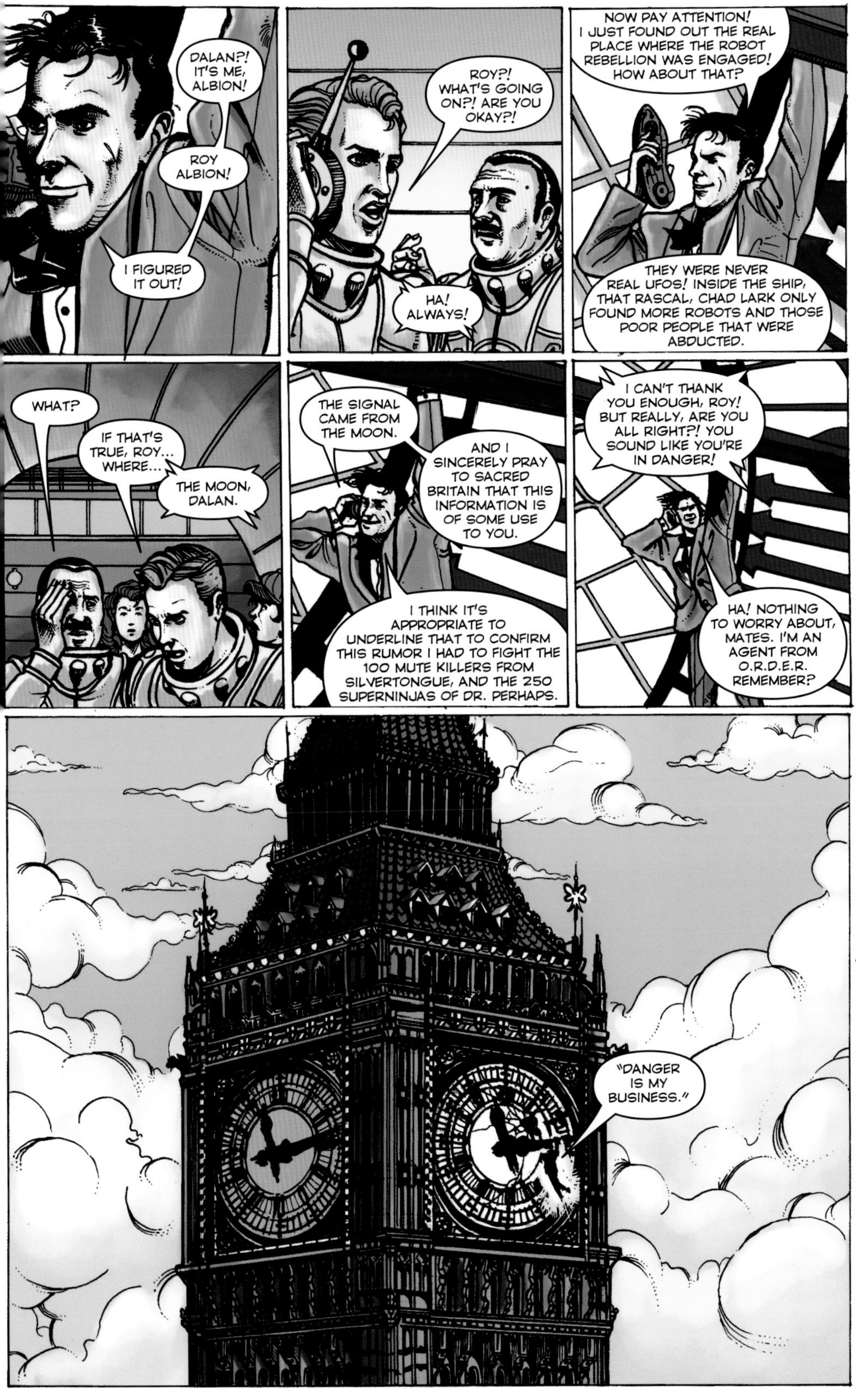
DALAN?! IT'S ME, ALBION!
ROY ALBION!
I FIGURED IT OUT!
ROY?! WHAT'S GOING ON?! ARE YOU OKAY?!
HA! ALWAYS!
NOW PAY ATTENTION! I JUST FOUND OUT THE REAL PLACE WHERE THE ROBOT REBELLION WAS ENGAGED! HOW ABOUT THAT?
THEY WERE NEVER REAL UFOS! INSIDE THE SHIP, THAT RASCAL, CHAD LARK ONLY FOUND MORE ROBOTS AND THOSE POOR PEOPLE THAT WERE ABDUCTED.
WHAT?
IF THAT'S TRUE, ROY... WHERE...
THE MOON, DALAN.
THE SIGNAL CAME FROM THE MOON.
AND I SINCERELY PRAY TO SACRED BRITAIN THAT THIS INFORMATION IS OF SOME USE TO YOU.
I THINK IT'S APPROPRIATE TO UNDERLINE THAT TO CONFIRM THIS RUMOR I HAD TO FIGHT THE 100 MUTE KILLERS FROM SILVERTONGUE, AND THE 250 SUPERNINJAS OF DR. PERHAPS.
I CAN'T THANK YOU ENOUGH, ROY! BUT REALLY, ARE YOU ALL RIGHT?! YOU SOUND LIKE YOU'RE IN DANGER!
HA! NOTHING TO WORRY ABOUT, MATES. I'M AN AGENT FROM O.R.D.E.R. REMEMBER?
"DANGER IS MY BUSINESS."

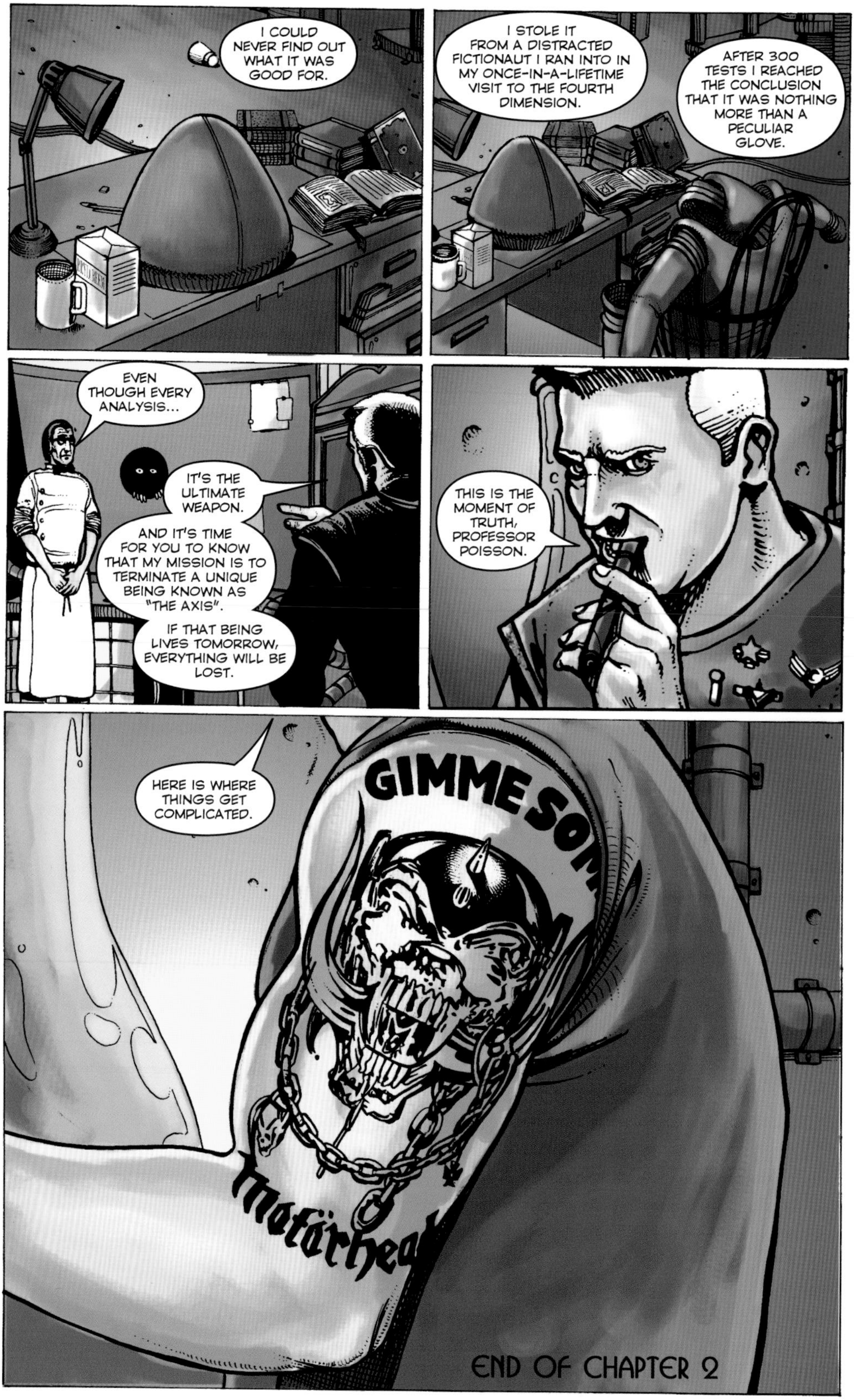
I COULD NEVER FIND OUT WHAT IT WAS GOOD FOR.
I STOLE IT FROM A DISTRACTED FICTIONAUT I RAN INTO IN MY ONCE-IN-A-LIFETIME VISIT TO THE FOURTH DIMENSION.
AFTER 300 TESTS I REACHED THE CONCLUSION THAT IT WAS NOTHING MORE THAN A PECULIAR GLOVE.
EVEN THOUGH EVERY ANALYSIS...
IT'S THE ULTIMATE WEAPON.
AND IT'S TIME FOR YOU TO KNOW THAT MY MISSION IS TO TERMINATE A UNIQUE BEING KNOWN AS "THE AXIS".
IF THAT BEING LIVES TOMORROW, EVERYTHING WILL BE LOST.
THIS IS THE MOMENT OF TRUTH, PROFESSOR POISSON.
HERE IS WHERE THINGS GET COMPLICATED.
END OF CHAPTER 2

# CHAPTER 3
# THE LAND THAT
# SPACE FORGOT!

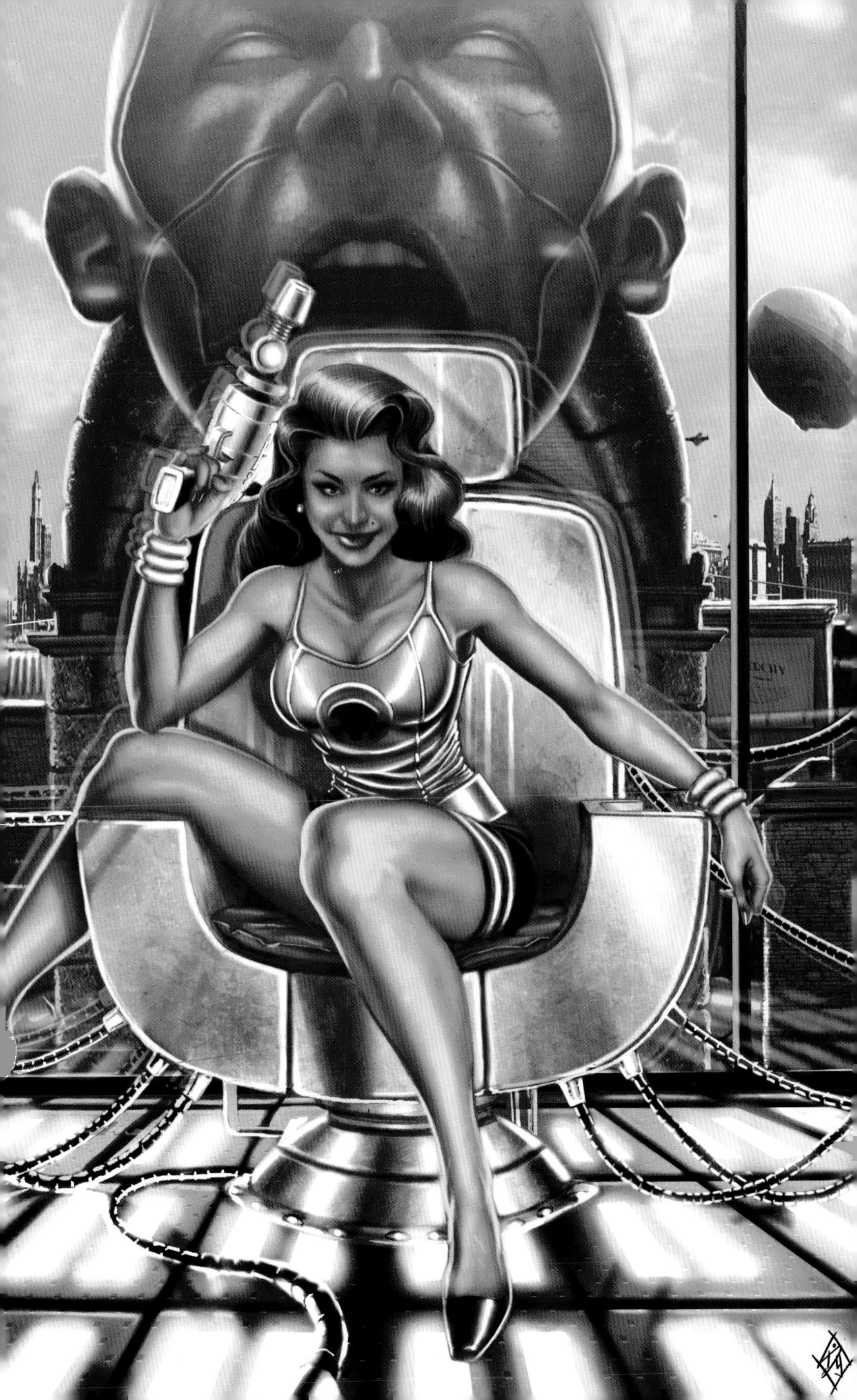

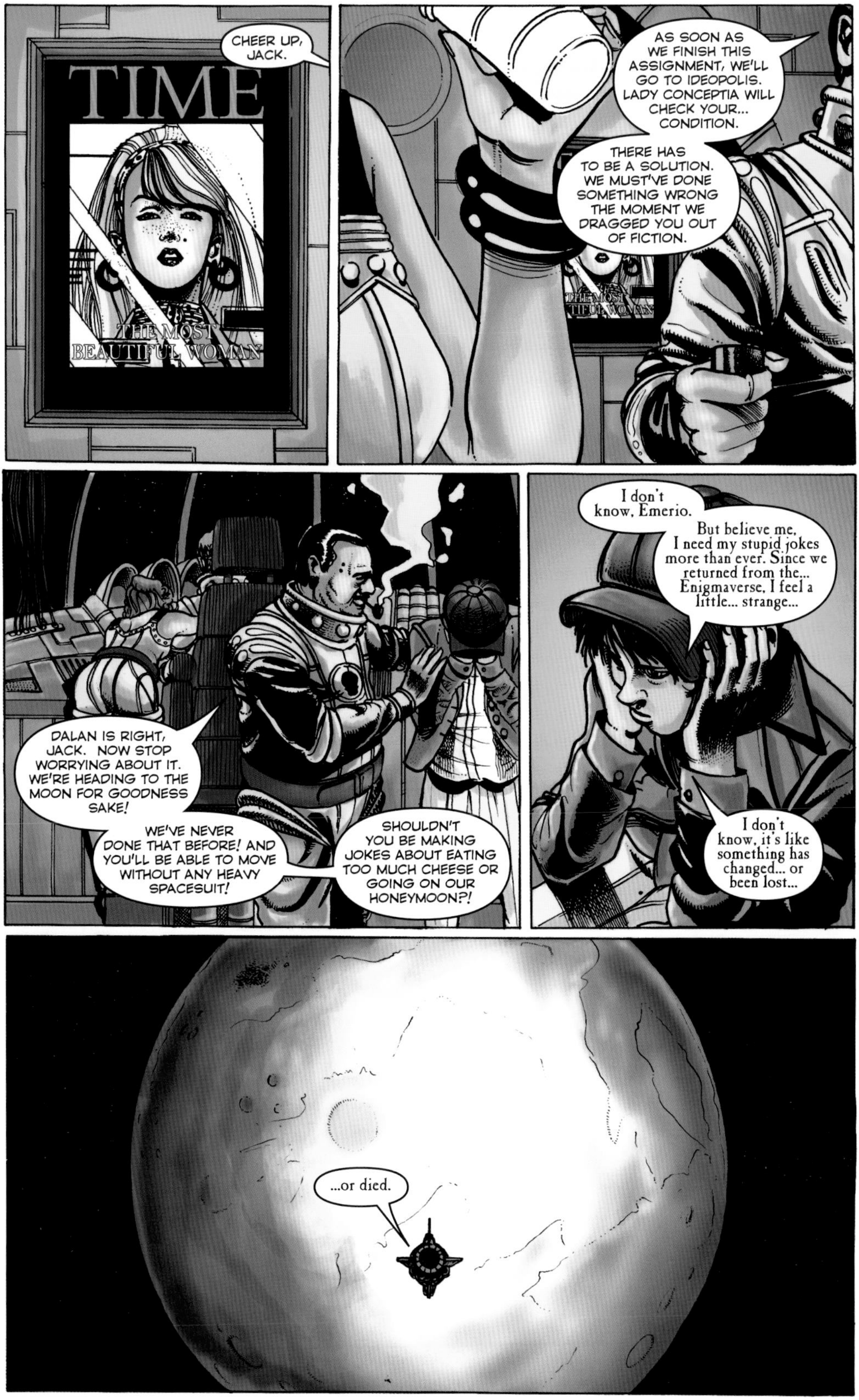
CHEER UP, JACK.
TIME
THE MOST BEAUTIFUL WOMAN
AS SOON AS WE FINISH THIS ASSIGNMENT, WE'LL GO TO IDEOPOLIS. LADY CONCEPTIA WILL CHECK YOUR... CONDITION.
THERE HAS TO BE A SOLUTION. WE MUST'VE DONE SOMETHING WRONG THE MOMENT WE DRAGGED YOU OUT OF FICTION.
DALAN IS RIGHT, JACK. NOW STOP WORRYING ABOUT IT. WE'RE HEADING TO THE MOON FOR GOODNESS SAKE!
WE'VE NEVER DONE THAT BEFORE! AND YOU'LL BE ABLE TO MOVE WITHOUT ANY HEAVY SPACESUIT!
SHOULDN'T YOU BE MAKING JOKES ABOUT EATING TOO MUCH CHEESE OR GOING ON OUR HONEYMOON?!
I don't know, Emerio.
But believe me, I need my stupid jokes more than ever. Since we returned from the... Enigmaverse, I feel a little... strange...
I don't know, it's like something has changed... or been lost...
...or died.

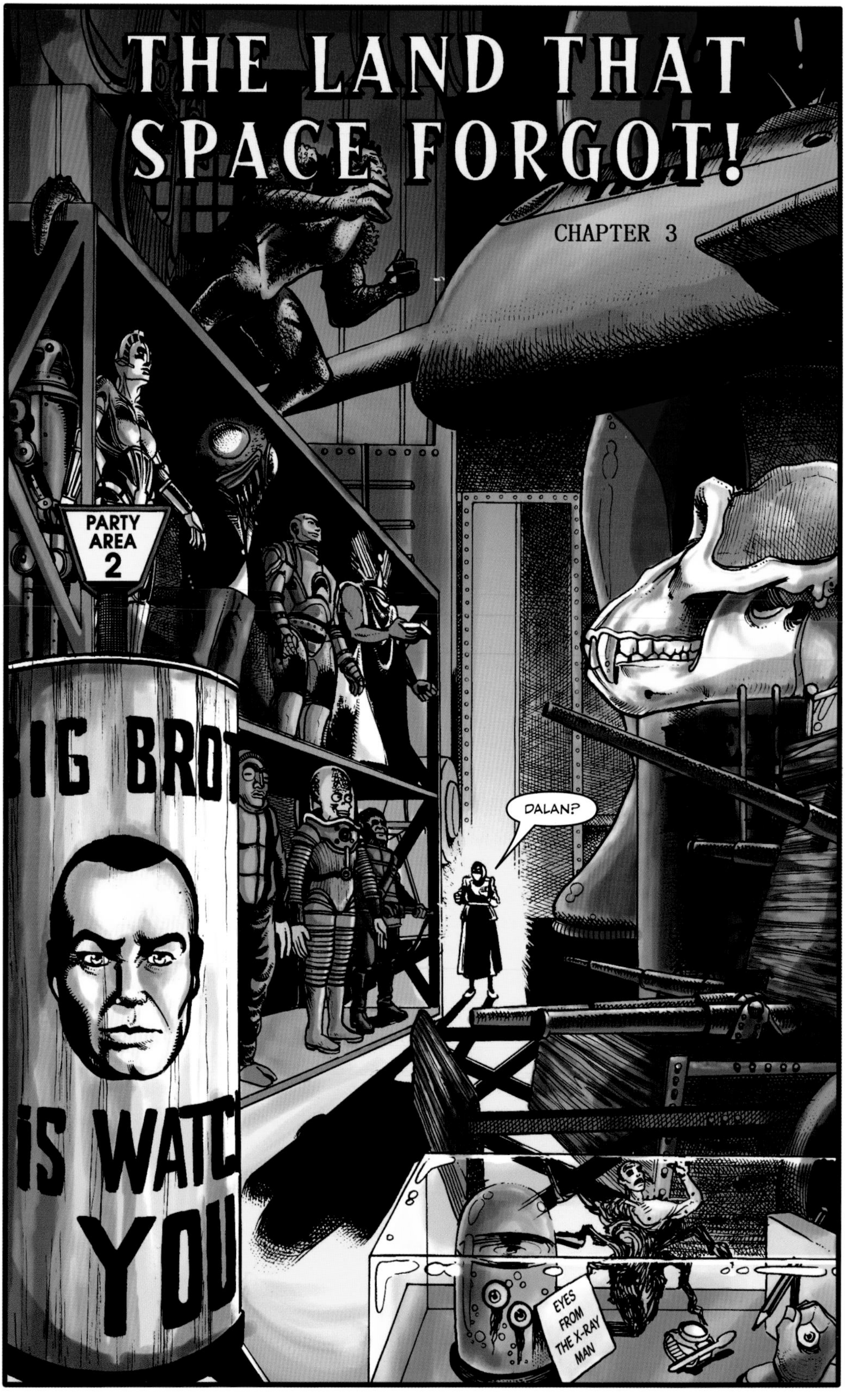
THE LAND THAT SPACE FORGOT!
CHAPTER 3
PARTY AREA 2
BIG BRO
IS WATC
YOU
DALAN?
EYES FROM THE X-RAY MAN

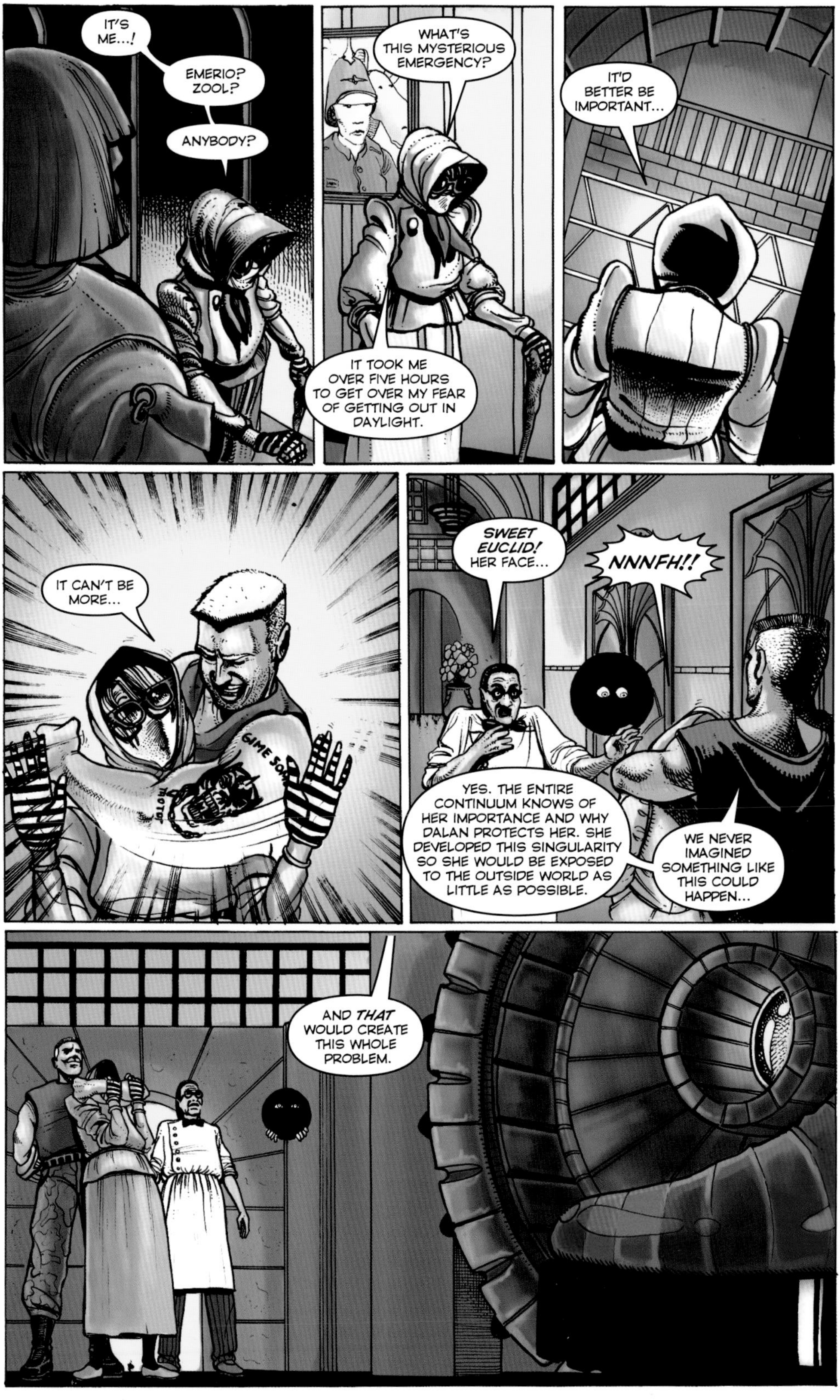
IT'S ME...!
EMERIO? ZOOL?
ANYBODY?
WHAT'S THIS MYSTERIOUS EMERGENCY?
IT TOOK ME OVER FIVE HOURS TO GET OVER MY FEAR OF GETTING OUT IN DAYLIGHT.
IT'D BETTER BE IMPORTANT...
IT CAN'T BE MORE...
SWEET EUCLID! HER FACE...
NNNFH!!
YES. THE ENTIRE CONTINUUM KNOWS OF HER IMPORTANCE AND WHY DALAN PROTECTS HER. SHE DEVELOPED THIS SINGULARITY SO SHE WOULD BE EXPOSED TO THE OUTSIDE WORLD AS LITTLE AS POSSIBLE.
WE NEVER IMAGINED SOMETHING LIKE THIS COULD HAPPEN...
AND THAT WOULD CREATE THIS WHOLE PROBLEM.

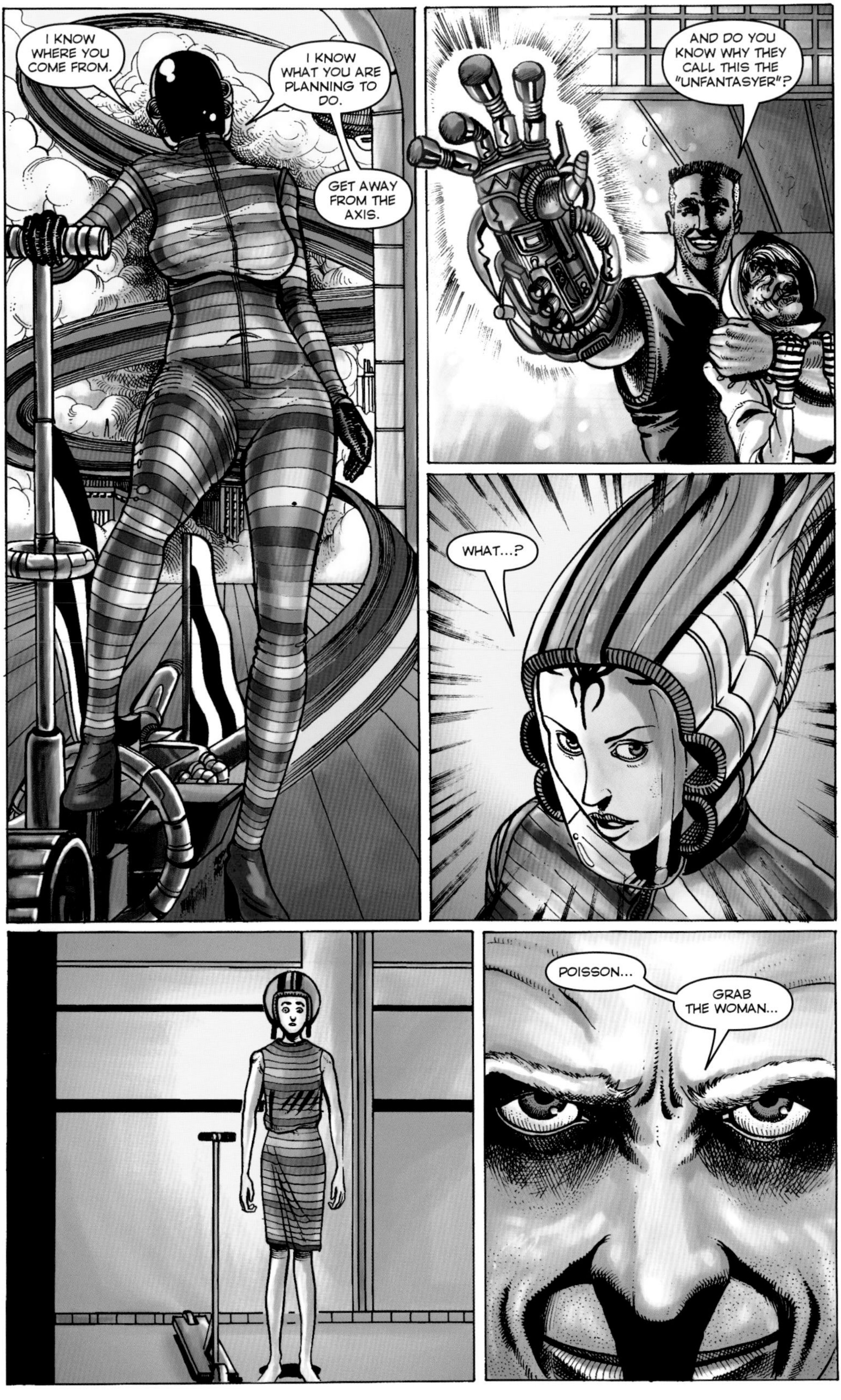
I KNOW WHERE YOU COME FROM.
I KNOW WHAT YOU ARE PLANNING TO DO.
GET AWAY FROM THE AXIS.
AND DO YOU KNOW WHY THEY CALL THIS THE "UNFANTASYER"?
WHAT...?
POISSON...
GRAB THE WOMAN...

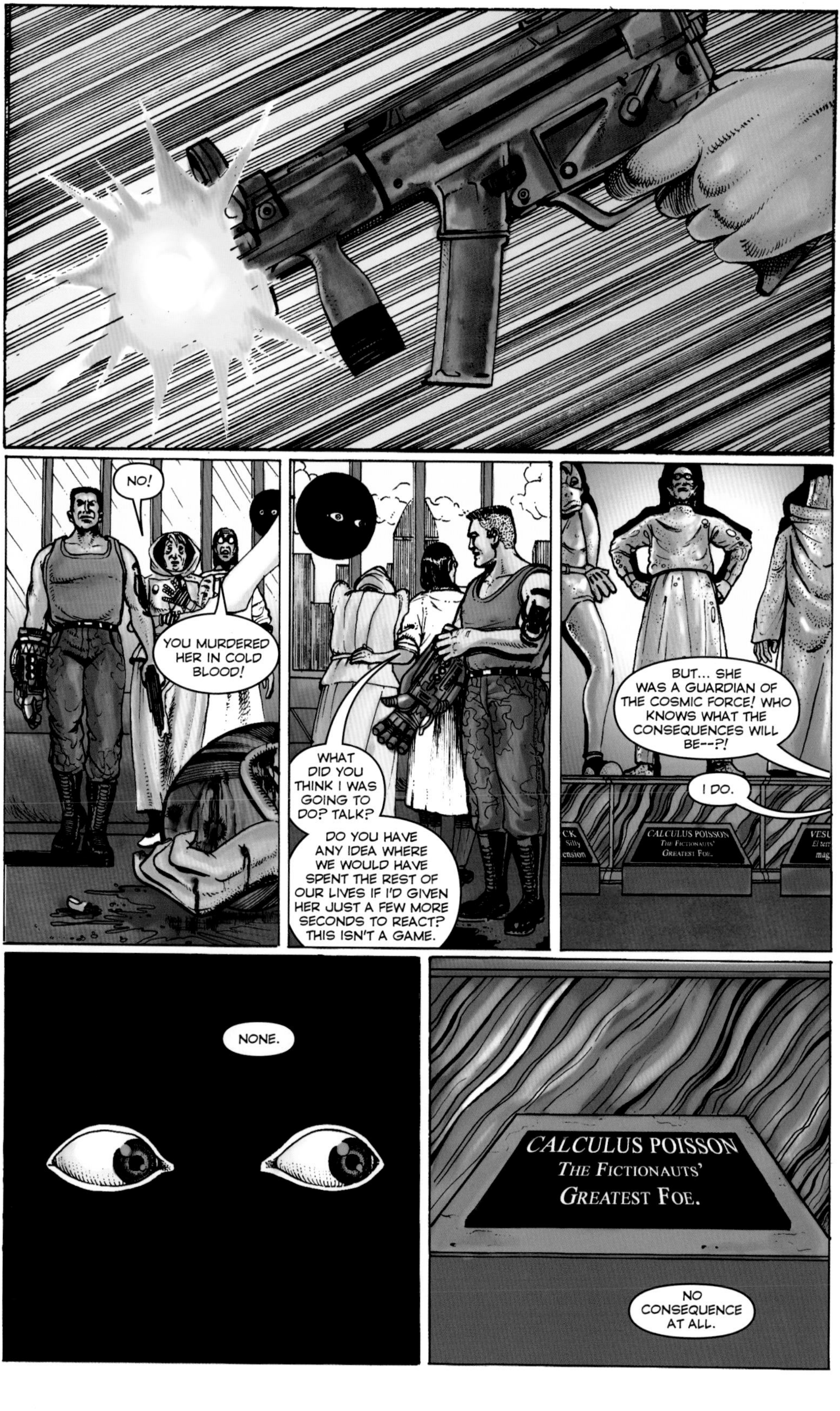
NO!
YOU MURDERED HER IN COLD BLOOD!
WHAT DID YOU THINK I WAS GOING TO DO? TALK?
DO YOU HAVE ANY IDEA WHERE WE WOULD HAVE SPENT THE REST OF OUR LIVES IF I'D GIVEN HER JUST A FEW MORE SECONDS TO REACT? THIS ISN'T A GAME.
BUT... SHE WAS A GUARDIAN OF THE COSMIC FORCE! WHO KNOWS WHAT THE CONSEQUENCES WILL BE--?!
I DO.
CALCULUS POISSON The Fictionauts' Greatest Foe.
NONE.
CALCULUS POISSON The Fictionauts' Greatest Foe.
NO CONSEQUENCE AT ALL.

ARE WE GOING TO DISCUSS IT OR NOT?

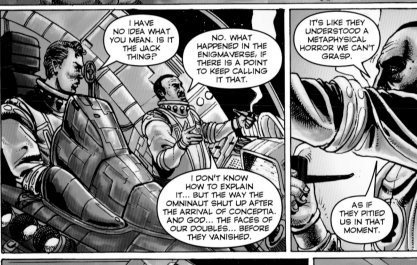

I HAVE NO IDEA WHAT YOU MEAN. IS IT THE JACK THING?

NO. WHAT HAPPENED IN THE ENIGMAVERSE, IF THERE IS A POINT TO KEEP CALLING IT THAT.

I DON'T KNOW HOW TO EXPLAIN IT... BUT THE WAY THE OMNINAUT SHUT UP AFTER THE ARRIVAL OF CONCEPTIA. AND GOD... THE FACES OF OUR DOUBLES... BEFORE THEY VANISHED.

IT'S LIKE THEY UNDERSTOOD A METAPHYSICAL HORROR WE CAN'T GRASP.

AS IF THEY PITIED US IN THAT MOMENT.

BUT IT DOESN'T MAKE ANY SENSE, THEY WERE JUST COPIES. LADY CONCEPTIA SAID THAT.

YOU DON'T THINK SHE WOULD LIE TO US... DO YOU?

I'D LIKE TO BELIEVE THAT, BUT...

THE PROBLEM IS THAT I JUST CONFIRMED THAT OKTAVIO ZEROCKS IS NOT IN JAIL. HE IS DYING OF POLIO IN AN ASYLUM.

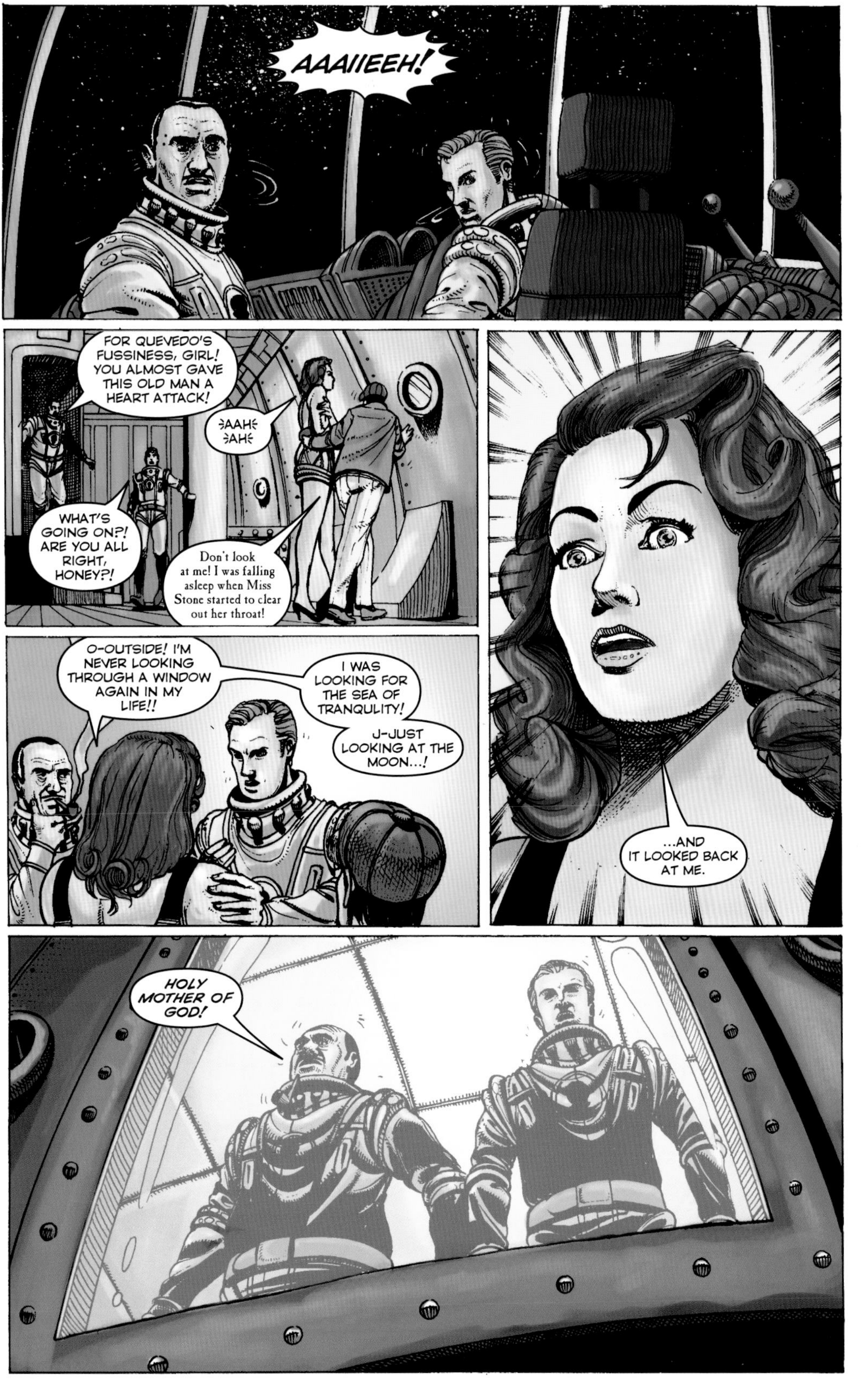
AAAIIEEH!
FOR QUEVEDO'S FUSSINESS, GIRL! YOU ALMOST GAVE THIS OLD MAN A HEART ATTACK!
AAH AH
WHAT'S GOING ON?! ARE YOU ALL RIGHT, HONEY?!
Don't look at me! I was falling asleep when Miss Stone started to clear out her throat!
O-OUTSIDE! I'M NEVER LOOKING THROUGH A WINDOW AGAIN IN MY LIFE!!
I WAS LOOKING FOR THE SEA OF TRANQULITY!
J-JUST LOOKING AT THE MOON...!
...AND IT LOOKED BACK AT ME.
HOLY MOTHER OF GOD!

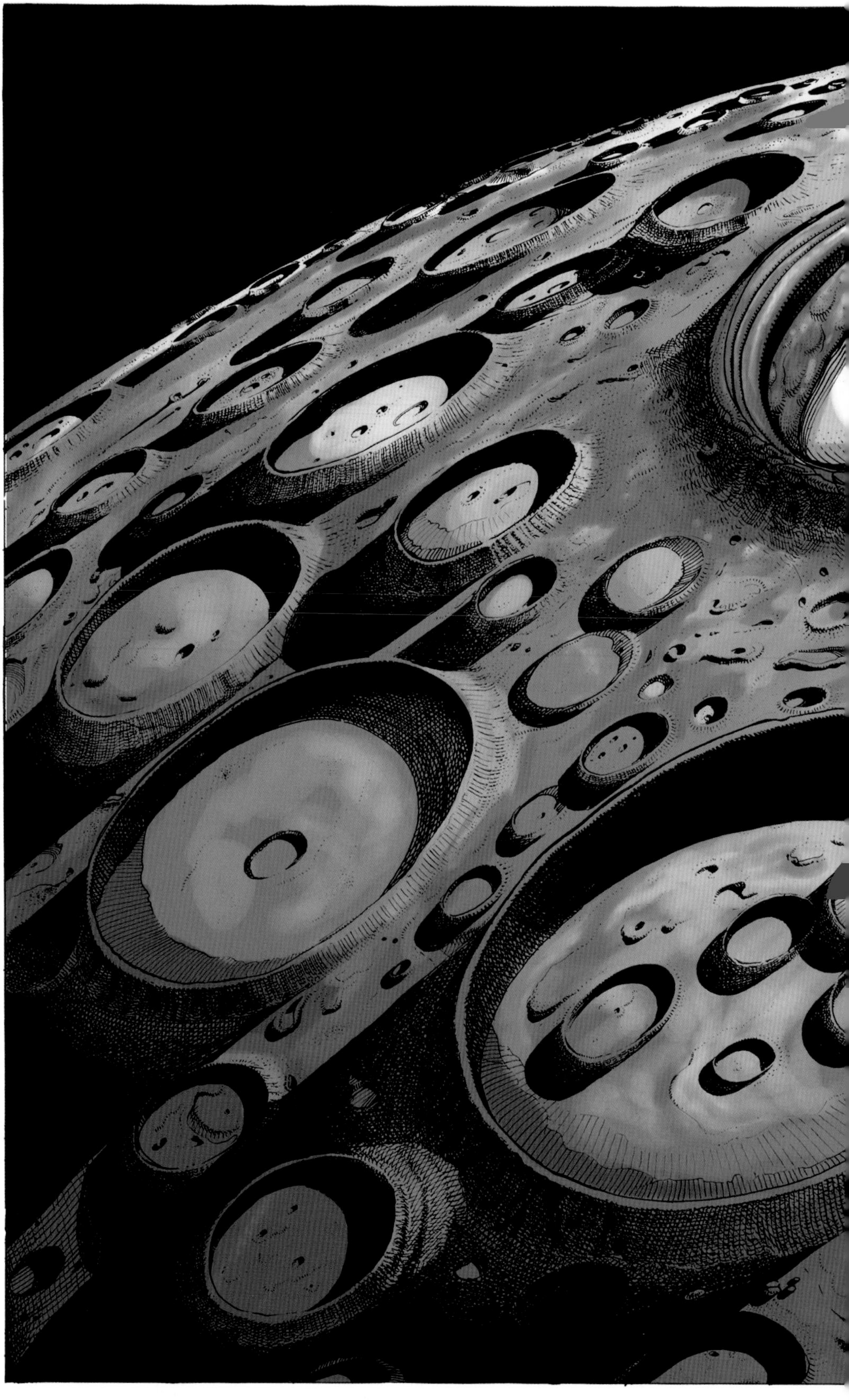

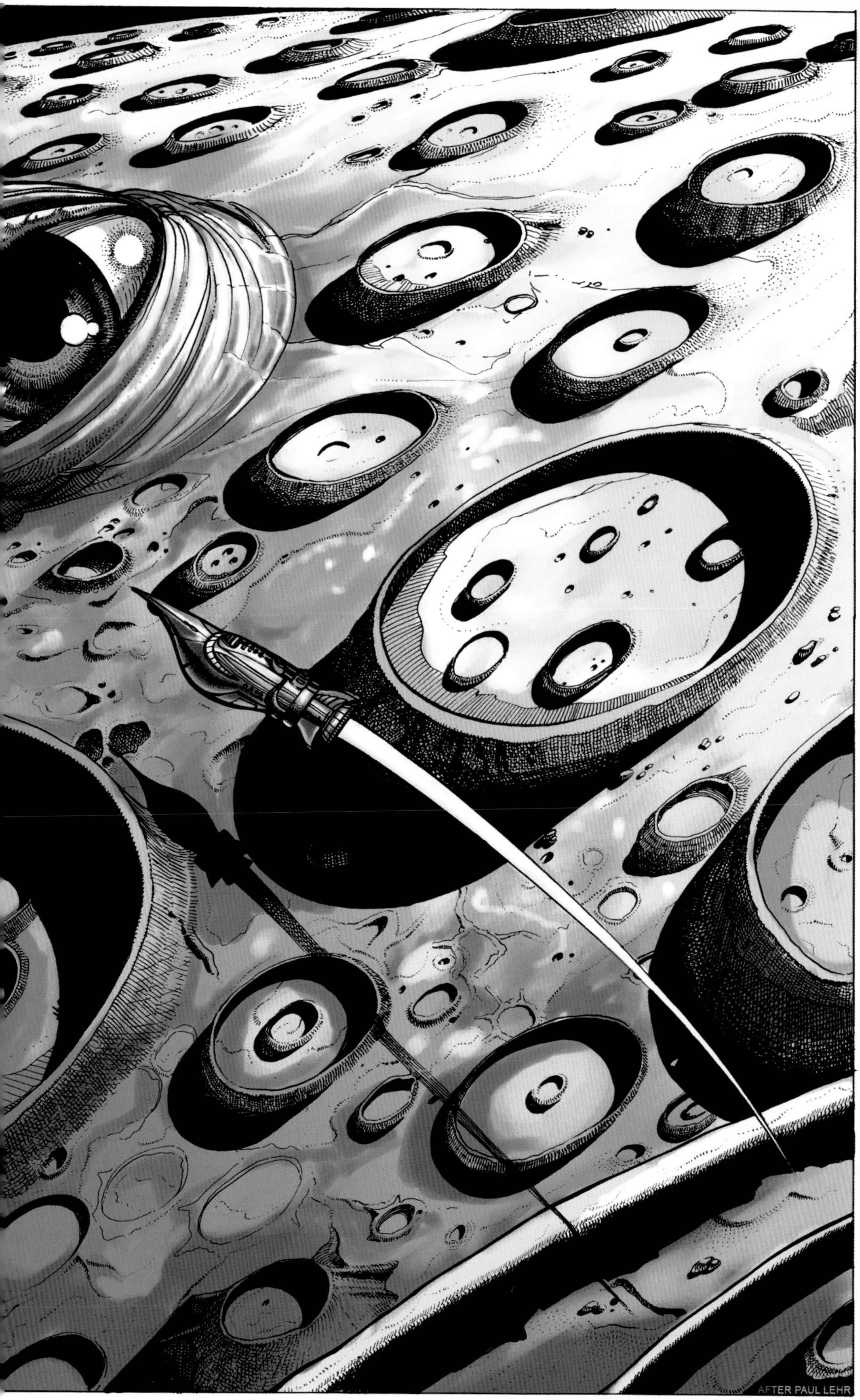
AFTER PAUL LEHR

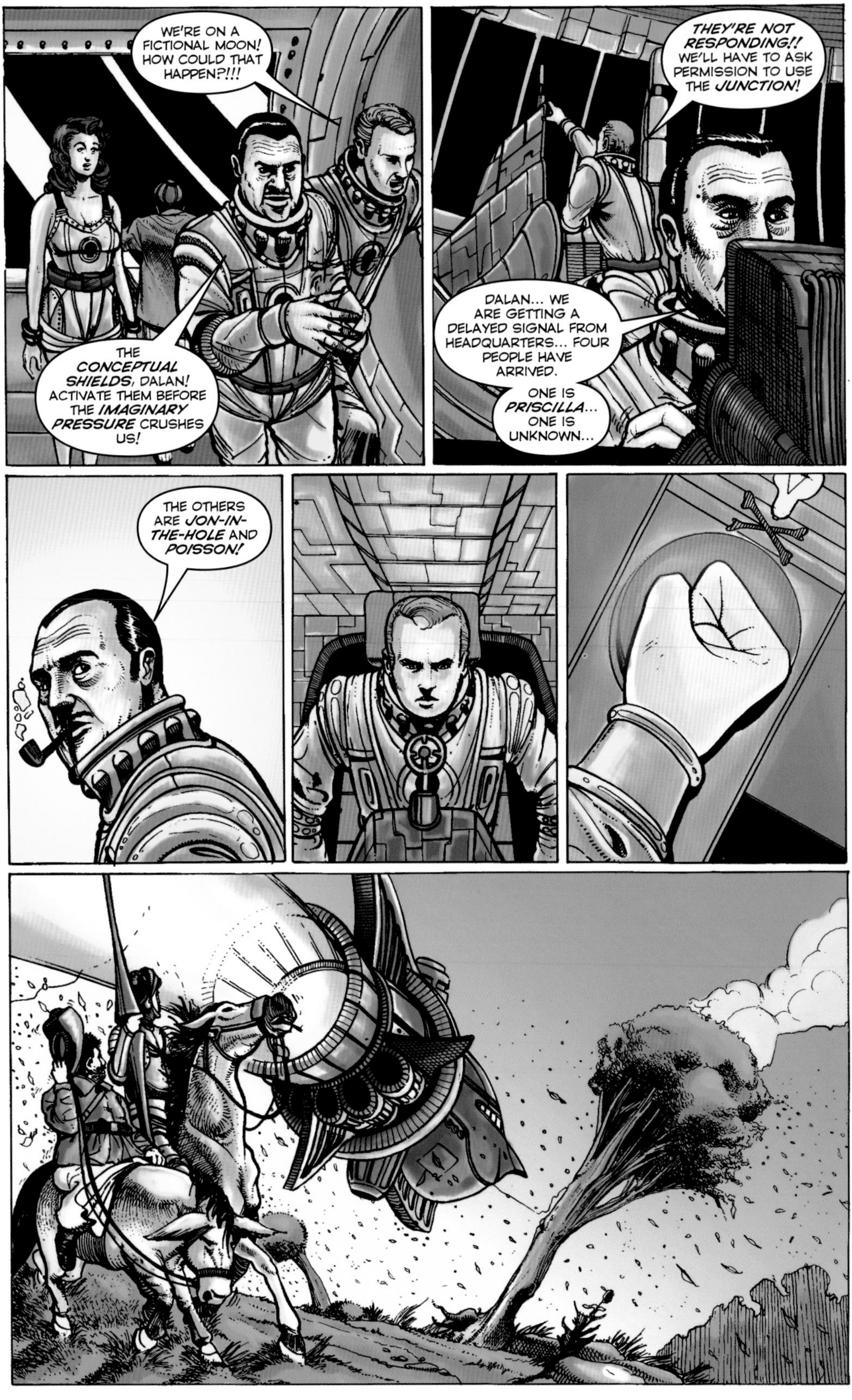
WE'RE ON A FICTIONAL MOON! HOW COULD THAT HAPPEN?!!!
THE CONCEPTUAL SHIELDS, DALAN! ACTIVATE THEM BEFORE THE IMAGINARY PRESSURE CRUSHES US!
THEY'RE NOT RESPONDING!! WE'LL HAVE TO ASK PERMISSION TO USE THE JUNCTION!
DALAN... WE ARE GETTING A DELAYED SIGNAL FROM HEADQUARTERS... FOUR PEOPLE HAVE ARRIVED.
ONE IS PRISCILLA... ONE IS UNKNOWN...
THE OTHERS ARE JON-IN-THE-HOLE AND POISSON!

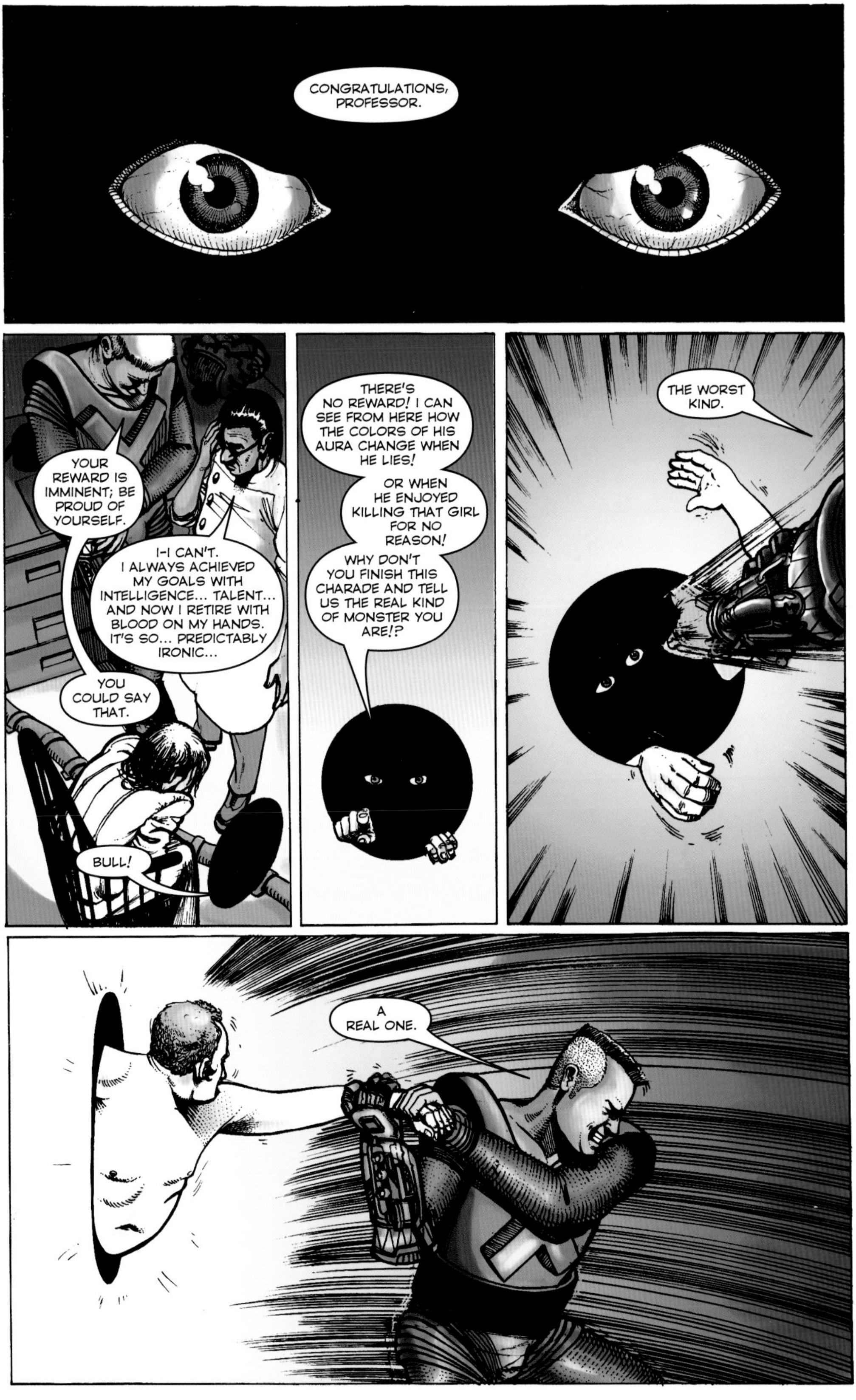
CONGRATULATIONS, PROFESSOR.
YOUR REWARD IS IMMINENT; BE PROUD OF YOURSELF.
I-I CAN'T. I ALWAYS ACHIEVED MY GOALS WITH INTELLIGENCE... TALENT... AND NOW I RETIRE WITH BLOOD ON MY HANDS. IT'S SO... PREDICTABLY IRONIC...
YOU COULD SAY THAT.
BULL!
THERE'S NO REWARD! I CAN SEE FROM HERE HOW THE COLORS OF HIS AURA CHANGE WHEN HE LIES!
OR WHEN HE ENJOYED KILLING THAT GIRL FOR NO REASON!
WHY DON'T YOU FINISH THIS CHARADE AND TELL US THE REAL KIND OF MONSTER YOU ARE!?
THE WORST KIND.
A REAL ONE.

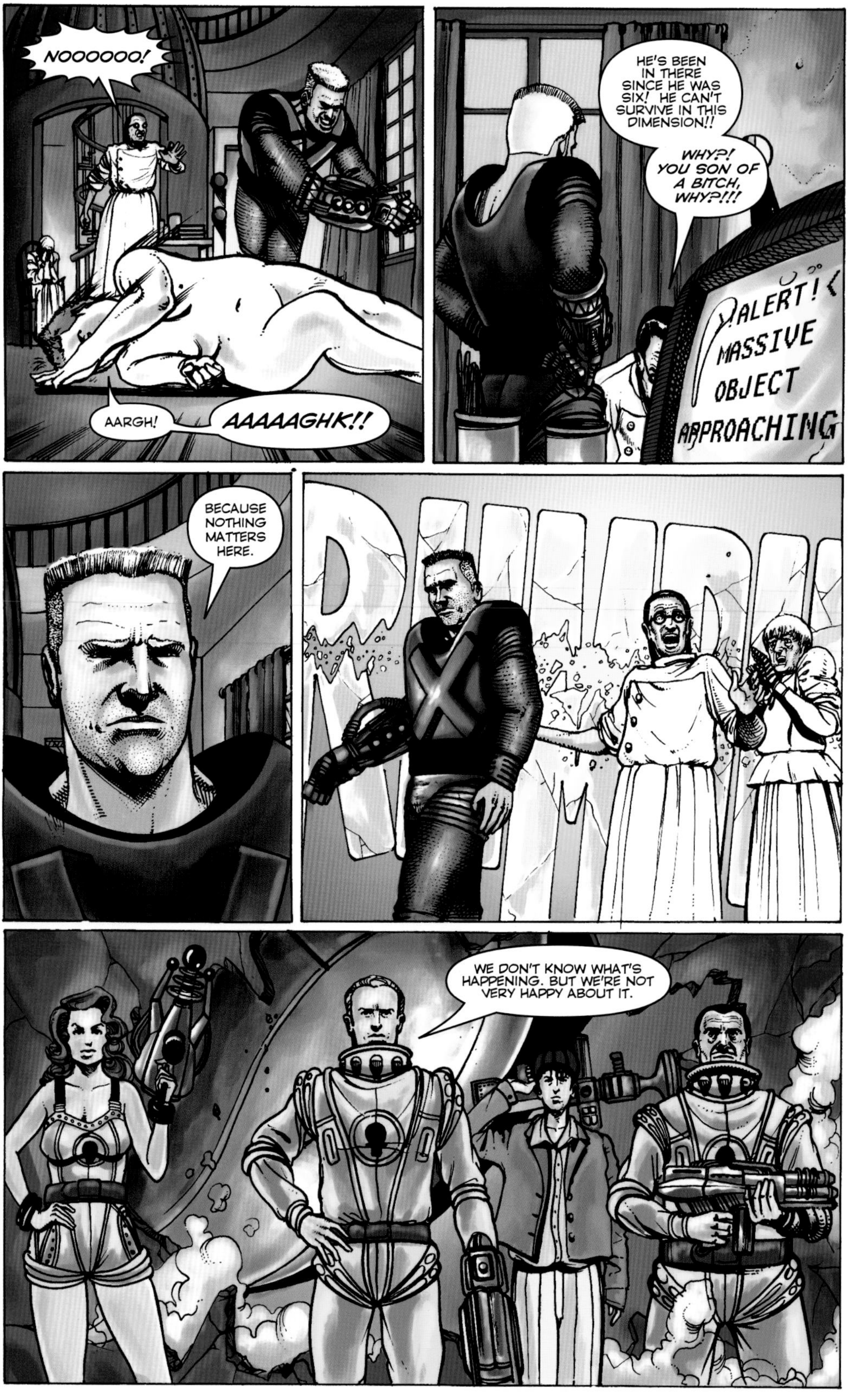
NOOOOOO!
AARGH!
AAAAAGHK!!
HE'S BEEN IN THERE SINCE HE WAS SIX! HE CAN'T SURVIVE IN THIS DIMENSION!!
WHY?! YOU SON OF A BITCH, WHY?!!!
ALERT! MASSIVE OBJECT APPROACHING
BECAUSE NOTHING MATTERS HERE.
WE DON'T KNOW WHAT'S HAPPENING. BUT WE'RE NOT VERY HAPPY ABOUT IT.

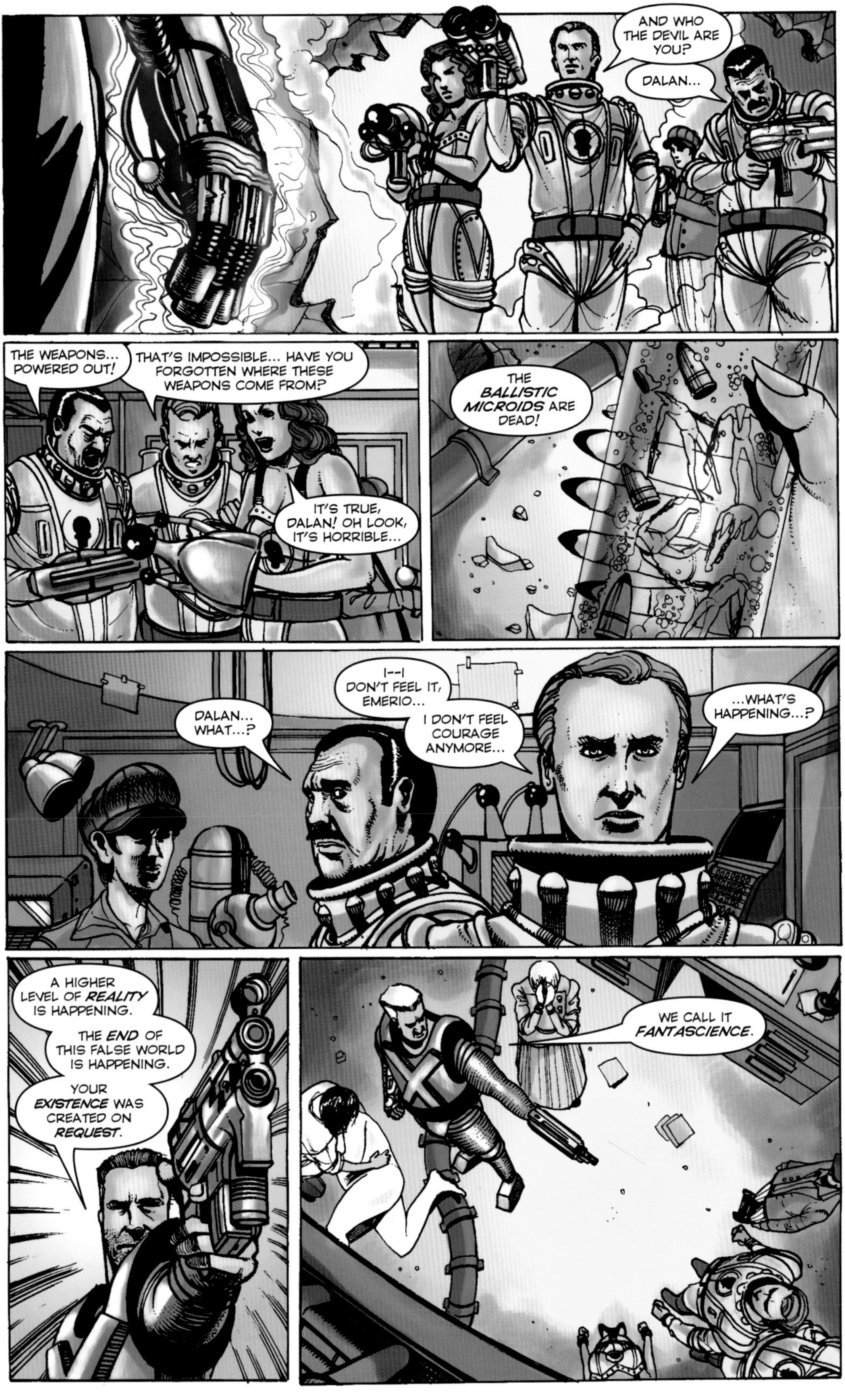
AND WHO THE DEVIL ARE YOU?
DALAN...
THE WEAPONS... POWERED OUT!
THAT'S IMPOSSIBLE... HAVE YOU FORGOTTEN WHERE THESE WEAPONS COME FROM?
IT'S TRUE, DALAN! OH LOOK, IT'S HORRIBLE...
THE BALLISTIC MICROIDS ARE DEAD!
DALAN... WHAT...?
I--I DON'T FEEL IT, EMERIO...
I DON'T FEEL COURAGE ANYMORE...
...WHAT'S HAPPENING...?
A HIGHER LEVEL OF REALITY IS HAPPENING.
THE END OF THIS FALSE WORLD IS HAPPENING.
YOUR EXISTENCE WAS CREATED ON REQUEST.
WE CALL IT FANTASCIENCE.

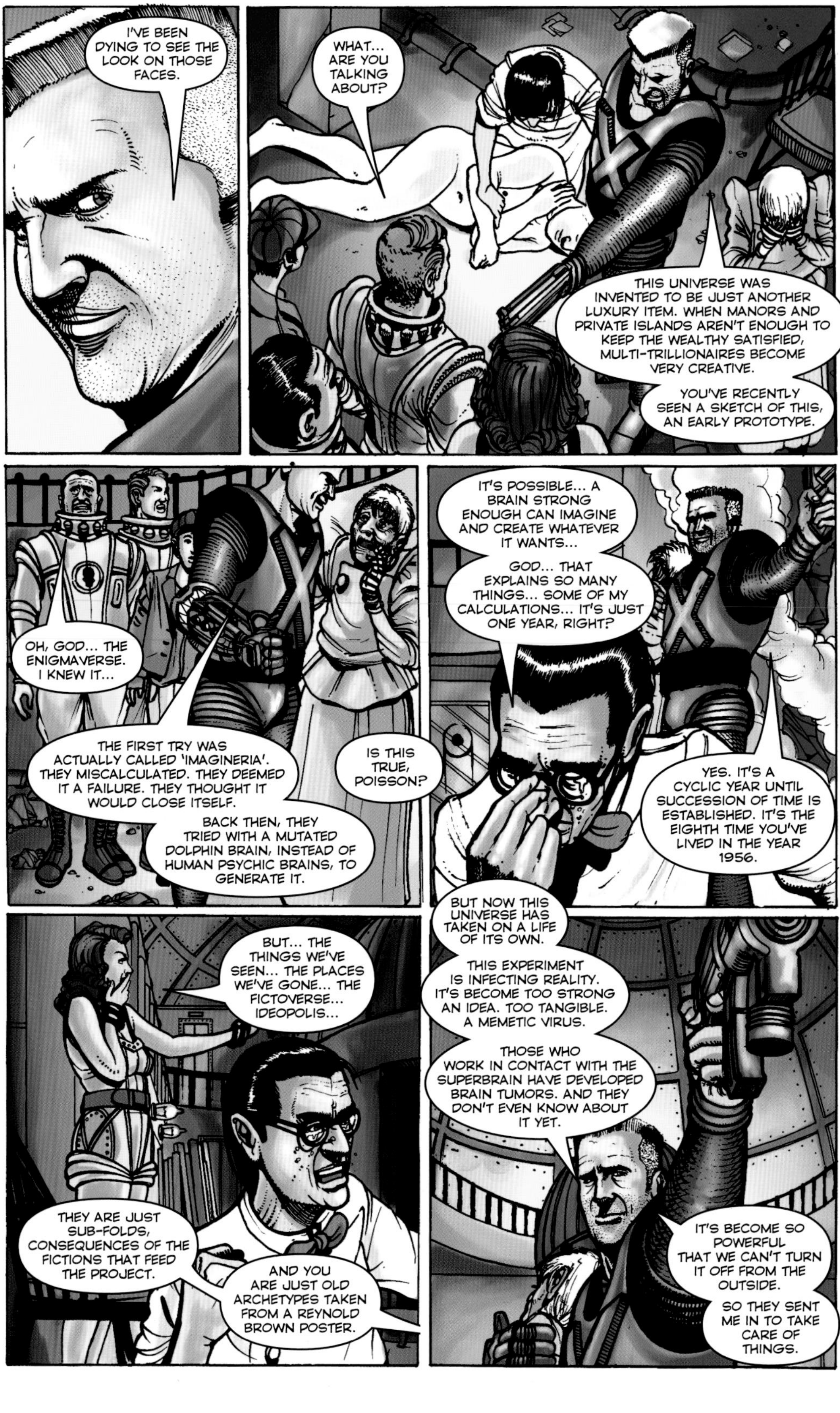
I'VE BEEN DYING TO SEE THE LOOK ON THOSE FACES.
WHAT... ARE YOU TALKING ABOUT?
THIS UNIVERSE WAS INVENTED TO BE JUST ANOTHER LUXURY ITEM. WHEN MANORS AND PRIVATE ISLANDS AREN'T ENOUGH TO KEEP THE WEALTHY SATISFIED, MULTI-TRILLIONAIRES BECOME VERY CREATIVE.
YOU'VE RECENTLY SEEN A SKETCH OF THIS, AN EARLY PROTOTYPE.
OH, GOD... THE ENIGMAVERSE. I KNEW IT...
THE FIRST TRY WAS ACTUALLY CALLED 'IMAGINERIA'. THEY MISCALCULATED. THEY DEEMED IT A FAILURE. THEY THOUGHT IT WOULD CLOSE ITSELF.
BACK THEN, THEY TRIED WITH A MUTATED DOLPHIN BRAIN, INSTEAD OF HUMAN PSYCHIC BRAINS, TO GENERATE IT.
IS THIS TRUE, POISSON?
IT'S POSSIBLE... A BRAIN STRONG ENOUGH CAN IMAGINE AND CREATE WHATEVER IT WANTS...
GOD... THAT EXPLAINS SO MANY THINGS... SOME OF MY CALCULATIONS... IT'S JUST ONE YEAR, RIGHT?
YES. IT'S A CYCLIC YEAR UNTIL SUCCESSION OF TIME IS ESTABLISHED. IT'S THE EIGHTH TIME YOU'VE LIVED IN THE YEAR 1956.
BUT... THE THINGS WE'VE SEEN... THE PLACES WE'VE GONE... THE FICTOVERSE... IDEOPOLIS...
THEY ARE JUST SUB-FOLDS, CONSEQUENCES OF THE FICTIONS THAT FEED THE PROJECT.
AND YOU ARE JUST OLD ARCHETYPES TAKEN FROM A REYNOLD BROWN POSTER.
BUT NOW THIS UNIVERSE HAS TAKEN ON A LIFE OF ITS OWN.
THIS EXPERIMENT IS INFECTING REALITY. IT'S BECOME TOO STRONG AN IDEA. TOO TANGIBLE. A MEMETIC VIRUS.
THOSE WHO WORK IN CONTACT WITH THE SUPERBRAIN HAVE DEVELOPED BRAIN TUMORS. AND THEY DON'T EVEN KNOW ABOUT IT YET.
IT'S BECOME SO POWERFUL THAT WE CAN'T TURN IT OFF FROM THE OUTSIDE.
SO THEY SENT ME IN TO TAKE CARE OF THINGS.

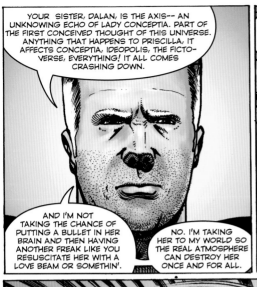

YOUR SISTER, DALAN, IS THE AXIS-- AN UNKNOWING ECHO OF LADY CONCEPTIA. PART OF THE FIRST CONCEIVED THOUGHT OF THIS UNIVERSE. ANYTHING THAT HAPPENS TO PRISCILLA, IT AFFECTS CONCEPTIA, IDEOPOLIS, THE FICTO-VERSE, EVERYTHING! IT ALL COMES CRASHING DOWN.

AND I'M NOT TAKING THE CHANCE OF PUTTING A BULLET IN HER BRAIN AND THEN HAVING ANOTHER FREAK LIKE YOU RESUSCITATE HER WITH A LOVE BEAM OR SOMETHIN'.

NO. I'M TAKING HER TO MY WORLD SO THE REAL ATMOSPHERE CAN DESTROY HER ONCE AND FOR ALL.

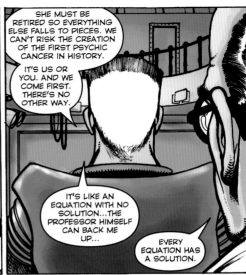

SHE MUST BE RETIRED SO EVERYTHING ELSE FALLS TO PIECES. WE CAN'T RISK THE CREATION OF THE FIRST PSYCHIC CANCER IN HISTORY.

IT'S US OR YOU. AND WE COME FIRST. THERE'S NO OTHER WAY.

IT'S LIKE AN EQUATION WITH NO SOLUTION...THE PROFESSOR HIMSELF CAN BACK ME UP...

EVERY EQUATION HAS A SOLUTION.

YOU JUST HAVE TO SORT OUT THE X.

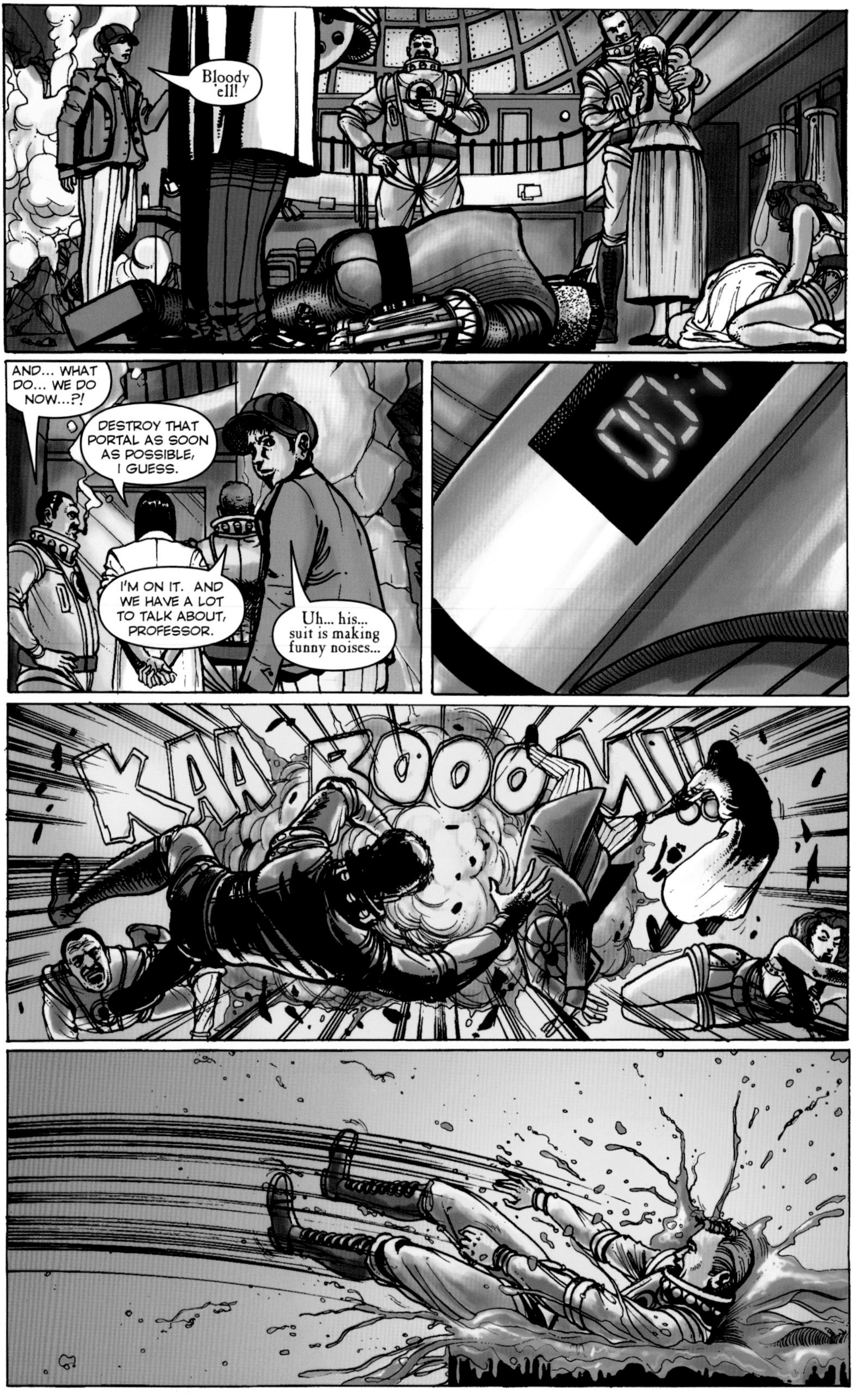
Bloody 'ell!
AND... WHAT DO... WE DO NOW...?!
DESTROY THAT PORTAL AS SOON AS POSSIBLE, I GUESS.
I'M ON IT. AND WE HAVE A LOT TO TALK ABOUT, PROFESSOR.
Uh... his... suit is making funny noises...
KAA-BOOOM!!

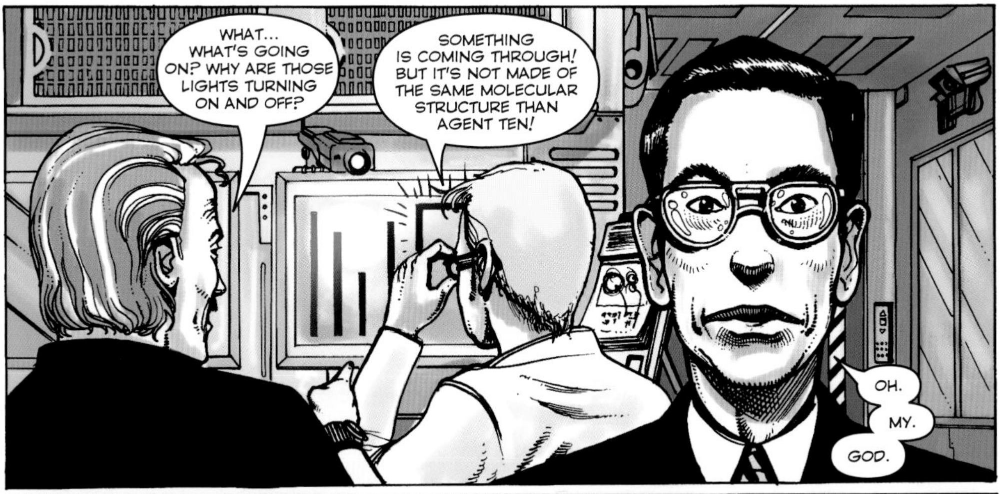
WHAT... WHAT'S GOING ON? WHY ARE THOSE LIGHTS TURNING ON AND OFF?
SOMETHING IS COMING THROUGH! BUT IT'S NOT MADE OF THE SAME MOLECULAR STRUCTURE THAN AGENT TEN!
OH.
MY.
GOD.
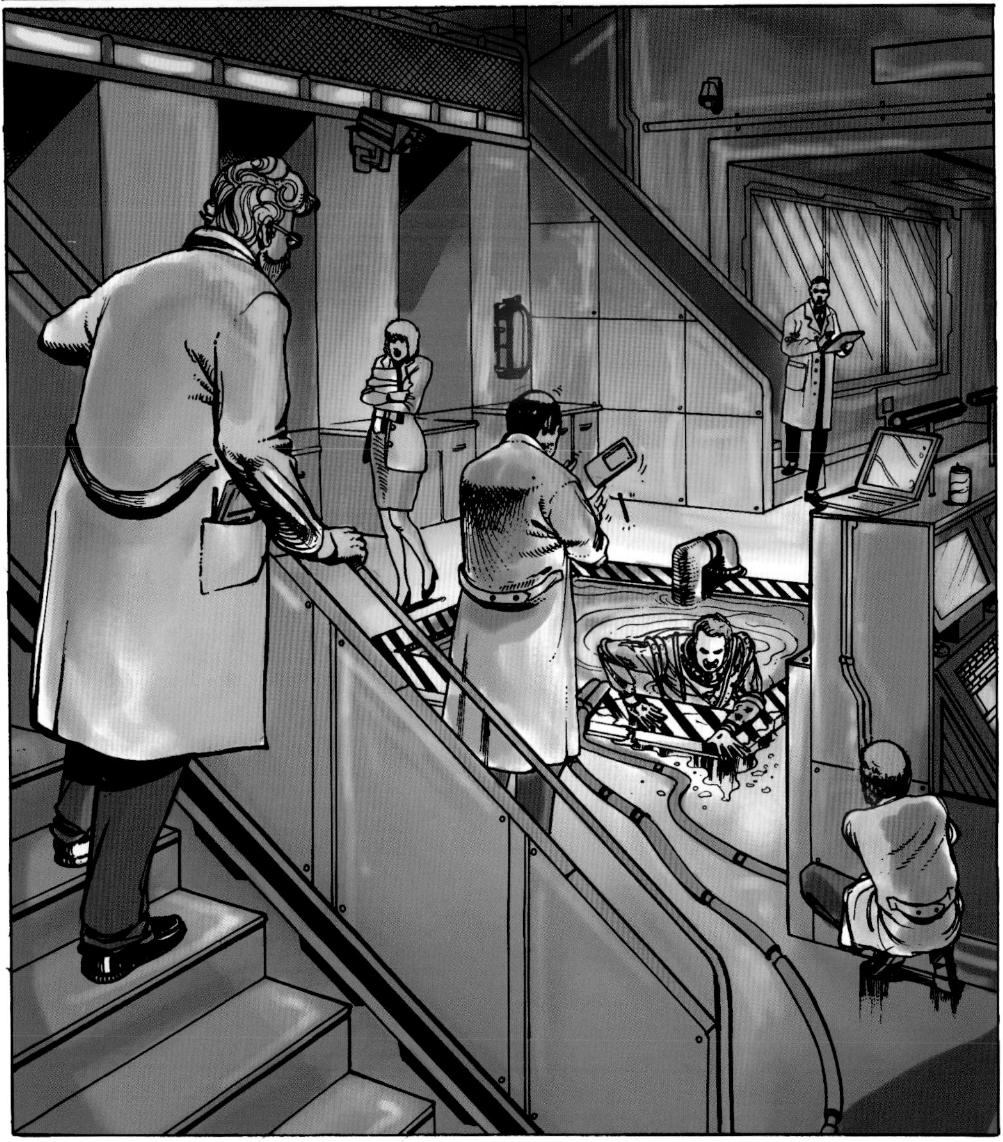

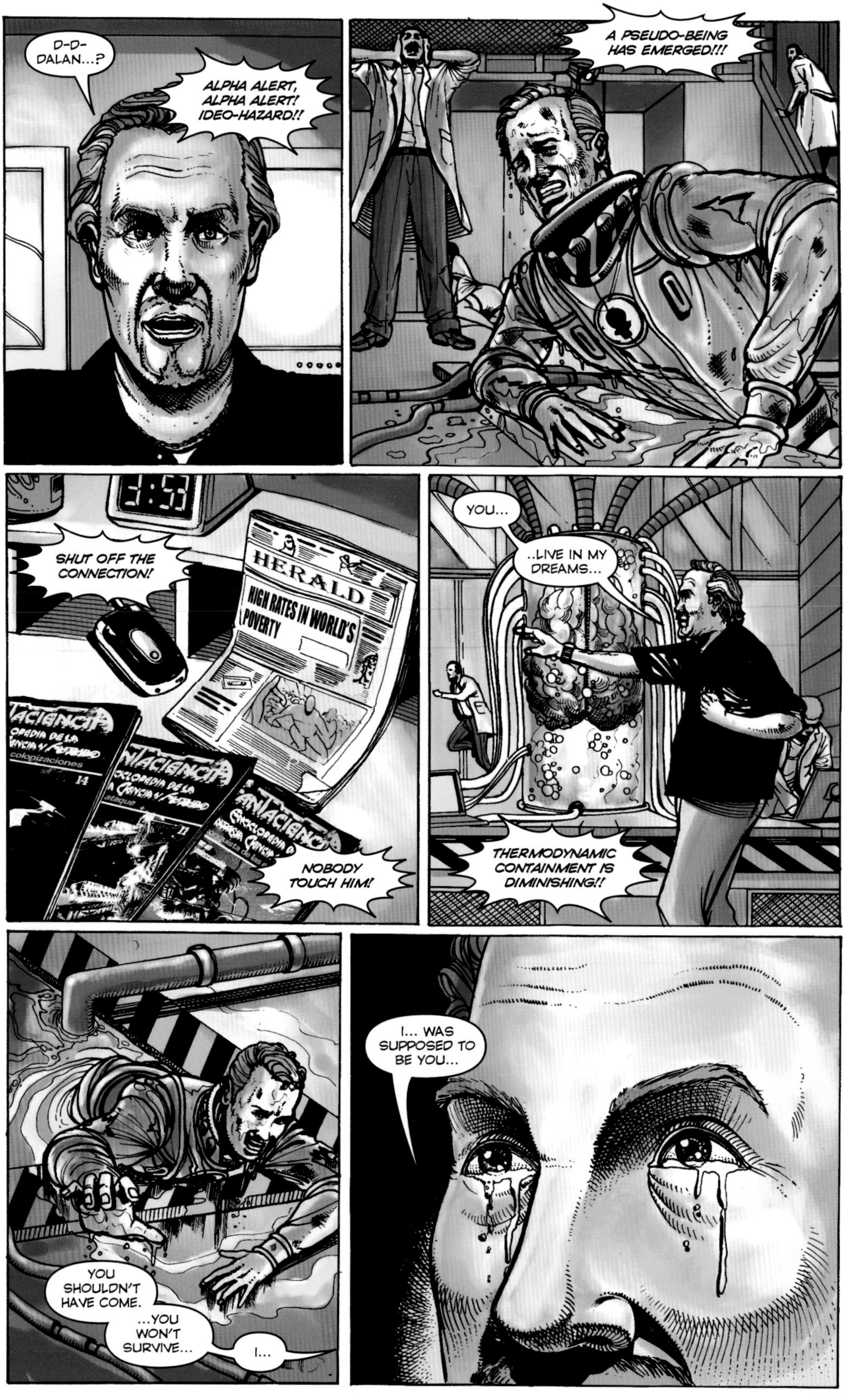
D-D-DALAN...?
ALPHA ALERT, ALPHA ALERT! IDEO-HAZARD!!
A PSEUDO-BEING HAS EMERGED!!!
SHUT OFF THE CONNECTION!
HERALD
HIGH RATES IN WORLD'S POVERTY
NOBODY TOUCH HIM!
YOU...
..LIVE IN MY DREAMS...
THERMODYNAMIC CONTAINMENT IS DIMINISHING!!
YOU SHOULDN'T HAVE COME.
...YOU WON'T SURVIVE...
I...
I... WAS SUPPOSED TO BE YOU...

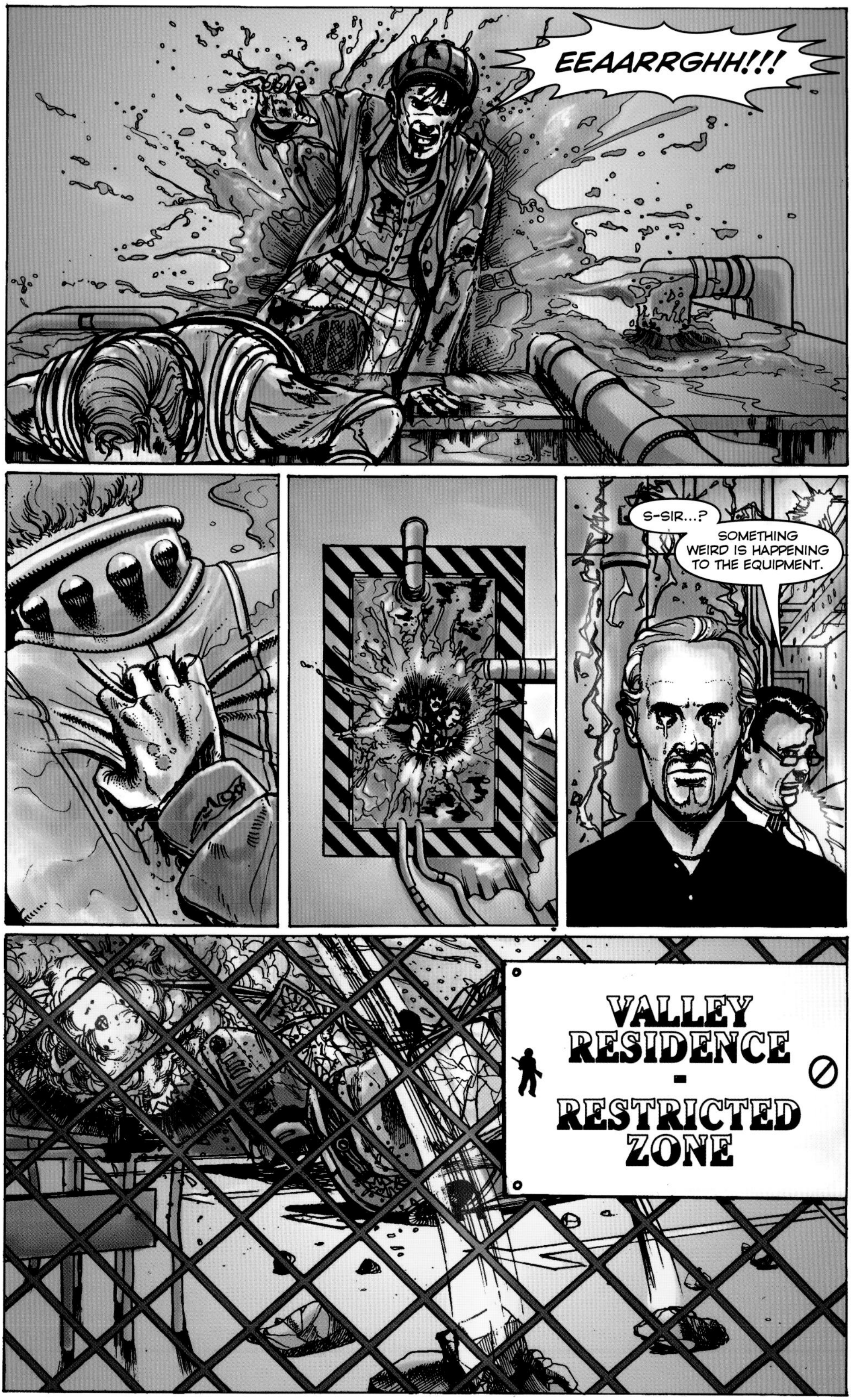
EEAARRGHH!!!
S-SIR...?
SOMETHING WEIRD IS HAPPENING TO THE EQUIPMENT.
VALLEY RESIDENCE - RESTRICTED ZONE

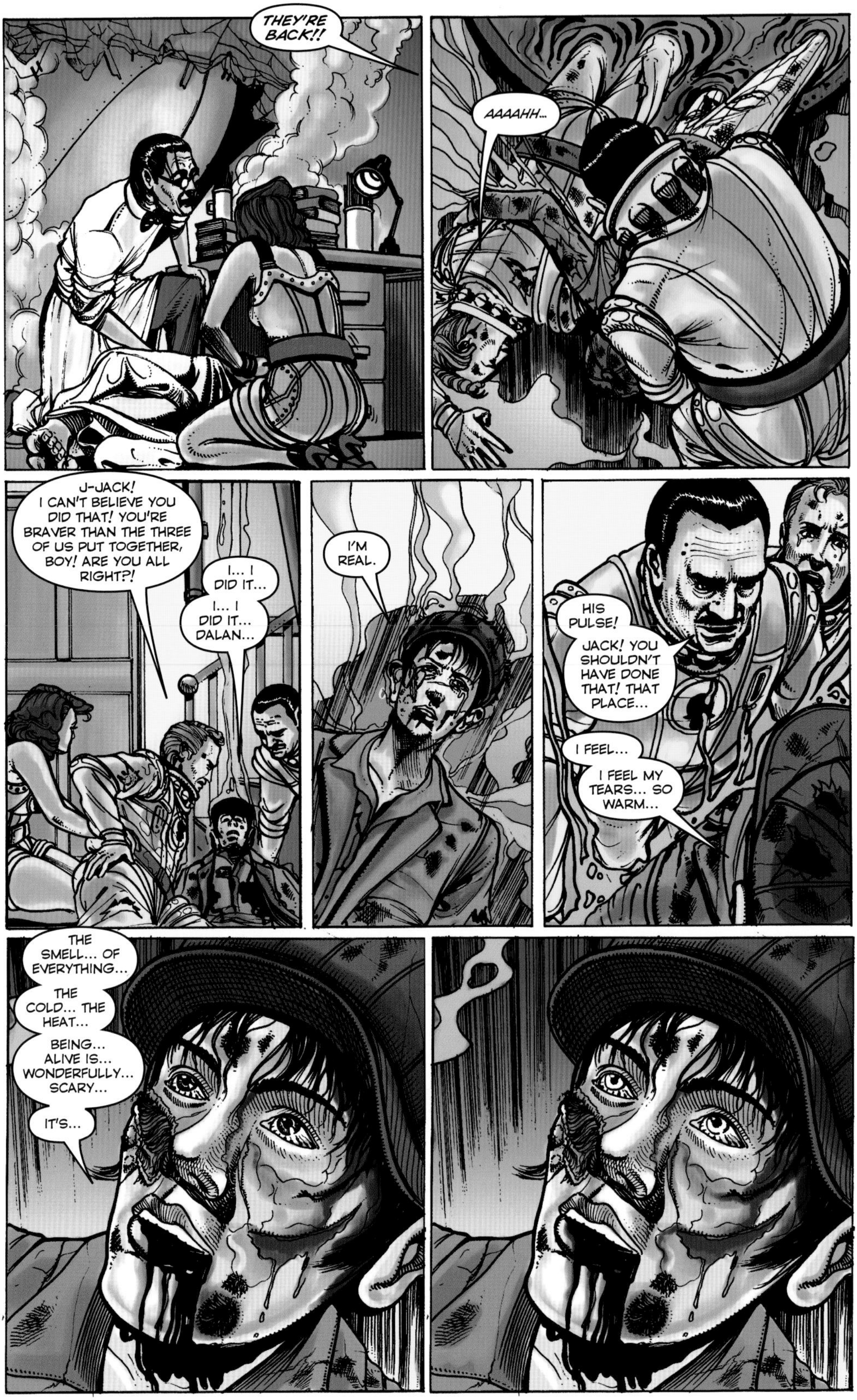
THEY'RE BACK!!
AAAAHH...
J-JACK! I CAN'T BELIEVE YOU DID THAT! YOU'RE BRAVER THAN THE THREE OF US PUT TOGETHER, BOY! ARE YOU ALL RIGHT?!
I... I DID IT...
I... I DID IT... DALAN...
I'M REAL.
HIS PULSE!
JACK! YOU SHOULDN'T HAVE DONE THAT! THAT PLACE...
I FEEL...
I FEEL MY TEARS... SO WARM...
THE SMELL... OF EVERYTHING...
THE COLD... THE HEAT...
BEING... ALIVE IS... WONDERFULLY... SCARY...
IT'S...

# Epilogue.

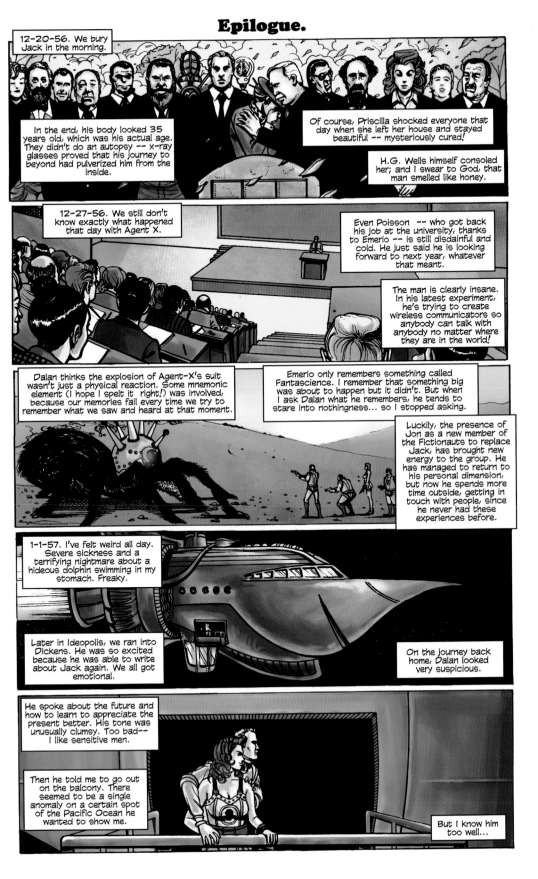

12-20-56. We bury Jack in the morning.

In the end, his body looked 35 years old, which was his actual age. They didn't do an autopsy -- x-ray glasses proved that his journey to beyond had pulverized him from the inside.

Of course, Priscilla shocked everyone that day when she left her house and stayed beautiful -- mysteriously cured!

H.G. Wells himself consoled her; and I swear to God, that man smelled like honey.

12-27-56. We still don't know exactly what happened that day with Agent X.

Even Poisson -- who got back his job at the university, thanks to Emerio -- is still disdainful and cold. He just said he is looking forward to next year, whatever that meant.

The man is clearly insane. In his latest experiment, he's trying to create wireless communicators so anybody can talk with anybody no matter where they are in the world!

Dalan thinks the explosion of Agent-X's suit wasn't just a physical reaction. Some mnemonic element (I hope I spelt it right!) was involved, because our memories fail every time we try to remember what we saw and heard at that moment.

Emerio only remembers something called Fantascience. I remember that something big was about to happen but it didn't. But when I ask Dalan what he remembers, he tends to stare into nothingness... so I stopped asking.

Luckily, the presence of Jon as a new member of the Fictionauts to replace Jack, has brought new energy to the group. He has managed to return to his personal dimension, but now he spends more time outside, getting in touch with people, since he never had these experiences before.

1-1-57. I've felt weird all day. Severe sickness and a terrifying nightmare about a hideous dolphin swimming in my stomach. Freaky.

Later in Ideopolis, we ran into Dickens. He was so excited because he was able to write about Jack again. We all got emotional.

On the journey back home, Dalan looked very suspicious.

He spoke about the future and how to learn to appreciate the present better. His tone was unusually clumsy. Too bad-- I like sensitive men.

Then he told me to go out on the balcony. There seemed to be a single anomaly on a certain spot of the Pacific Ocean he wanted to show me.

But I know him too well...

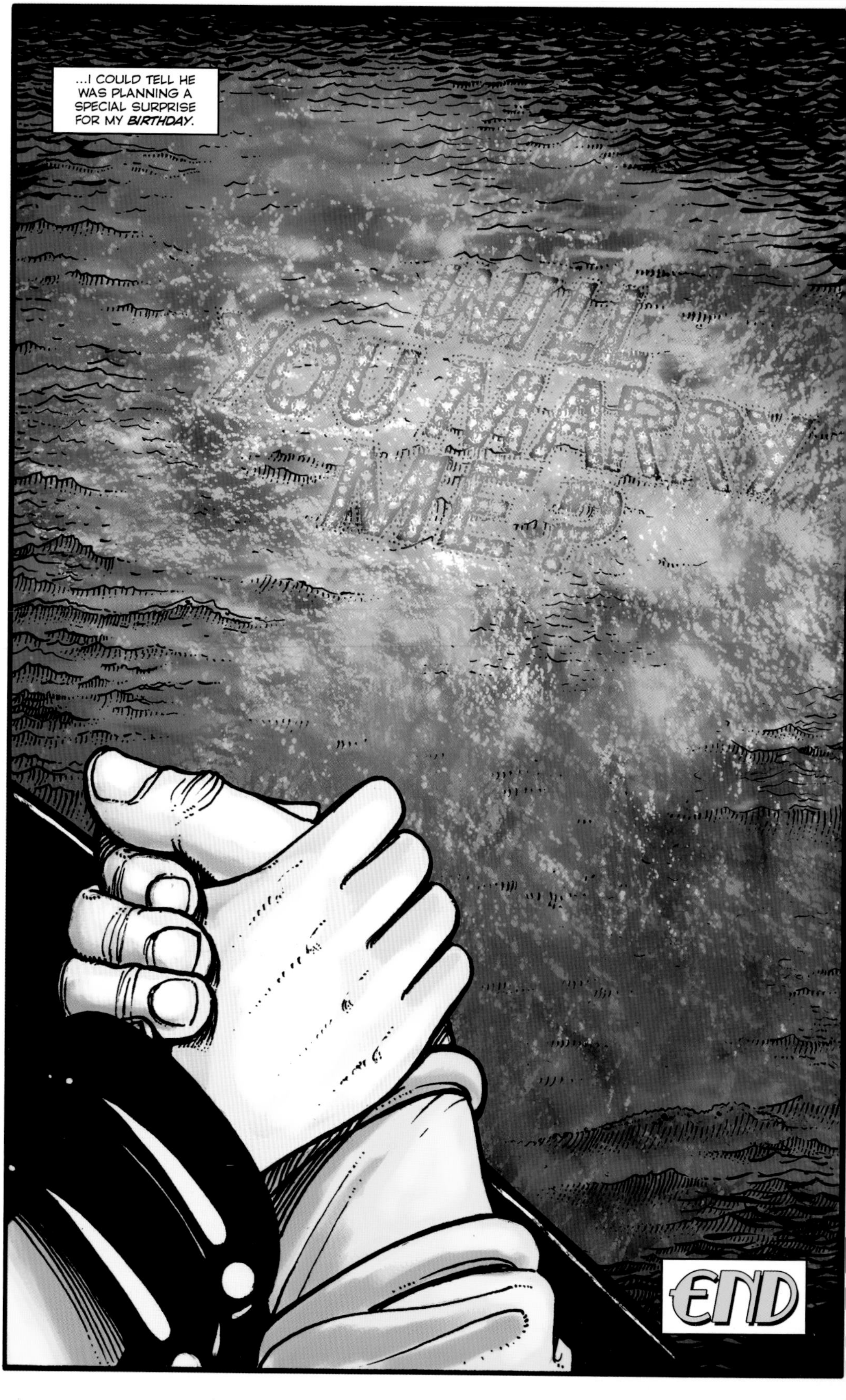
...I COULD TELL HE WAS PLANNING A SPECIAL SURPRISE FOR MY *BIRTHDAY*.
WILL YOU MARRY ME?
END